I0733530

KHAAK

THE MESSAGE

KHAAK
THE MESSAGE

Mahdi

Published by IML Publications LLC in conjunction with Global Voice®
www.imlpublications.com; www.globalvoicefoundation.com

Distributed worldwide by Ingram Content Group
www.ingramcontent.com

Book cover artwork 'Timeless Eye of Eternity by Nuha
Book cover graphic and Interior layout by Zhaoying Zhu

ISBN: 978-1-955314-29-9 (paperback)
ISBN: 978-1-955314-30-5 (e-book)

Library of Congress Control Number: 2023906511

IML Publications LLC
151 First Avenue
New York City, NY 10003

To ALLAH (AL Qadir Mutlaq) for putting the Message in.

To Prophet Muhammad (ﷺ) for putting the Light in.

To Mothers, for putting the Love in.

To Children, for putting the Courage in.

To You---

-for putting the Meaning in...

My mother; to you, for giving me life

My ishq and my kids; to you, for giving me a world brimming

with pure magic & irrevocable love

To Al-Khidr; to you O noble murshid, for setting me free

As-salamu alaykum

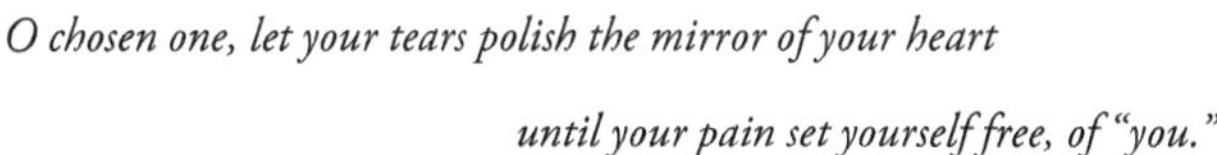

O chosen one, let your tears polish the mirror of your heart

until your pain set yourself free, of "you."

"BE" without your "Being"

The Divine Zaat awaits

To those on the path….

all **suffering** *is "grace"*

I would shake the dust from my coat

and rise if I realized my own perfection.

I would rush to the sky, empty and light;

My head would be high as the ninth heaven.

Rumi, Kolliyaat-e Shams-e Tabrizi

AUTHOR'S NOTE

Khaak is a work of fiction, inspired by the heinous attack on the Army Public School in Peshawar, Pakistan that took the lives of more than 144 children and adults by the Terrorist organization called TTP(Tehrik-i-Taliban) on December 16, 2014. Space and time in the novel have been rearranged to suit the convenience of the book. Certain long-standing institutions, agencies, and public offices are mentioned, but the characters involved are wholly imaginary. Any resemblance to anyone living or dead is purely coincidental. The opinions expressed are those of the characters and should not be confused with the author's.

Writing *Khaak* was a conscious decision. I wanted to create a story-world that didn't necessarily begin with screams and end in silence. But involved a growing presence, the presence of a message that has not been said, but which is very much there. The story does not intend to present things through the cold-eyed lens of factuality, rather it encourages you to listen to the voice of the unspoken and the unsullied.

As the author of the book, I think the enormity of what's happened in APS Peshawar is far too powerful a black void -- a maelstrom -- and a far too great looming presence in the daily lives of the people living there. The parents are still beating their wounds, and there are people literally walking around still suffering, both physically and psychosomatically wounded. Ultimately, one surely hopes for a day when there are stories, songs, and happiness coming out of all corners of the world that have nothing to do with the painful realities of war and terrorism. But there is a long way to go as the story of life is unfolding a grievous yet jarring truth for humanity to witness; tactical warfare, premeditated displacement and brutal murder of children and innocent people in various parts of the world. It's far too great a reality to turn away from.

This story therefore is a shout out to the broken hearts, to let them know that their pain is not only seen but felt intensely, in the entire echelon of the readers' being, even if it is through a fictitious lens and the APS arc.

It is also imperative for the readers to understand that any association or fervor represented in the story pertaining to any organization, person or idea is purely reflective of the characters and their respective personality and the cultural arc and is rudimentary for the development of the narrative itself.

At the end, the story is not preaching to the audience to pick sides, blame or extol an institution or establish a prejudice against the other. Rather, it accentuates the message of unity and oneness when it comes to the human existence and purpose of life. *Khaak* brings these questions to the forefront: Didn't we create the war, the conflicts and consequently, the terrorists? Didn't we choose sides and give in to the illusion of 'us' versus 'them'? Didn't we initiate and co-create nationalistic fervor, weapons and armies to topple universal balance in the name of "defense" "religion" and "patriotism"? Look around you, the Earth is morphing into Hades because we willfully choose victim consciousness every day.

Whether one sees into the mirror or the one reflected in the mirror sees you—isn't that the same image? Separation stems from looking at everything from the outside and everyone as the "other." How do we begin to look from the inside out instead of the outside in? This story is not channeling that separation, rather it is calling all readers to dive in and be eternally present concurrently on both sides, and yet be neither. Then only *Khaak*'s message will extend and unravel itself beyond the polarity.

The story is intended to offer the grieving true hope, to live again, to rise from their pain and reach a certain level of peace, with and without. The story also intends to pay tribute to the martyred children and adults, lost to war and violence of all sorts that they shall not be forgotten. The story intends to mark their sacrifices in indelible ink, on the pages of time and eternity; so long as the words exist, their image shall not be blotted out of existence.

Khaak also serves as a reminder that the struggles and scars of the people in Waziristan, Afghanistan, and of those displaced by war in Palestine and/or any part of the world is a real time human tragedy. For further explanation of words in Urdu, as well as Pashto, the local dialects of the Pashtuns and Afghans, please refer to the Glossary in the back of the book.

PROLOGUE

He looked up at the date—December 16, 2014—and wondered if the world would remember this day. Would they remember this day and all those days when innocent children like him lay sprawled like broken dolls, their joy stilled forever for a crime they never committed? Or would those left behind simply perform their vigils, cry a little, and then forget them all? Would they remember, Zufash wondered?

The children's uneven breathing filtered quietly through the silence, as the clock in the classroom chimed eleven o'clock. The only other sound was the wind, as it sighed mournfully through the line of trees that circled the school, as if lamenting the loss of innocence, the loss of humanity. Zufash opened his eyes and turned his head to stare toward the glow of the morning light. It seemed so dark, and he could scarcely distinguish the window from the walls of his classroom. As he endeavored to pierce that darkness with his dimming eyes, he made a thoughtful wish, on quivering lips and halting speech: "May you never forget; may you never forgive; O Allah! Remember me, remember us. Remember our pain." And HE did remember . . .

Alas, the world forgot.

A STAR LOST IN TIME

December 2001.

Location: Datta Khel, North Waziristan

Ten-year-old Bahadur stood on a pine-clad spur of the mountain, glancing over the forested slopes while his herd of sheep grazed on the summer grass covering the wide plateau as fleecy white clouds moved overhead. Ahead, the green valley spread out like a heavenly panorama, widening into a large plain where, nestled between the peaks and hidden within their folds, the rolling river bordered Datta Khel, his village of mud and stone. Partially hidden within groves of mulberry and walnuts, Datta Khel sat tucked among the lower spurs of the mountains.

Farther down the hills, on either side, the land closed tightly, becoming rugged and bare. Here, the river wound its circuitous path through the gorge, debouching upon terraced green fields of corn and chili, where his sheep could graze for endless hours of the day and where few people were ever seen. And yet, despite this, for Bahadur, this was the best evidence of life—soundless, only the man and the steady breeze, dancing, and gusting in praise to this godly heaven he called home.

His land, so much like a scrap hemmed to the threadbare boundaries of Pakistan, overlapping the Afghan frontier across the Preghal mount range. His father told him there was a time when no borderline was imprinted into the sand by the military men or imprinted with ink to paper. The blood of others could never cut deep enough to tear apart the drapery of the Waziri lineage. It came first, before all else. Even the outside world pronounced Waziristan in strange accents. It was the golden bastion of Islam. And it meant . . . *everything*. His Baba would always say to him,

"You are a *Wazir*, my son, God sent a mighty lion to Tibet, making its ferocious mouth the guardian of the brave." His Baba would point at the boy, at a young Bahadur. "You came from that mouth. And, my son, that is why I named you . . . *Bahadur*."

Never once did Bahadur doubt that myth, not even for a moment. Though he did not understand the true meaning of it as a child, he knew it meant a great deal indeed, in his small, tucked-away corner of the world. He grew quickly, adhering strictly to the Pashtunwali code of honor, following his ancestral laws of the tribe. One of these laws, one his Baba would mention often, as if by way of instruction, was that Bahadur was to stand tall against the enemy.

Subjugation was disgraceful. His Baba, Zaram Khan, was the master of the family and the senior member of the tribal Jirga in Datta Khel. He came across as a formidable man, and yet also compassionate; plain-spoken, with an innate understanding of the rights of those around him and the ability to judge; accordingly, a man the people trusted and respected irrefutably. Enormous responsibility lay upon his shoulders, for his role was the maintenance of discipline in the tribe, as he advised and watched over the young, keeping the family together and ensuring that all were treated fairly.

Bahadur not only loved his Baba beyond any doubt, but he also admired him. He would look up at the man's thickly muscled torso and his strong limbs, hear his powerful voice that thundered out from a place of truth and filled the boy with an irrefutable affection. For Bahadur, there was a simple truth in knowing where he belonged, in his home, amongst his people and his land.

As the winter sun climbed toward noon, he knew it was time

to go home. He flocked his herd, their continual braying like the sound of air caught in a broken pipe organ. He did not want his Mor[1] to become upset. She never approved of his shepherding, not until he reached the age of ten. Until then, she thought him too young. She also knew him well, that he would find it tiresome being on the hillside with only sheep for company. He'd find ways to amuse himself, running up rocks, rushing through the peaks, climbing trees, chasing birds, and trapping butterflies. He loved the idea of being in the wilderness, accompanied by long strips of cloud in the wide green valley, instead of being confined to his quiet speck of a village. He was like a bird, new to its flight, yearning to fly above the trees and into the sky to live amongst the stars—that is, until his longing for his Mor would overpower all other desires and he returned to the nest.

The gilded crest of the clouds began to form above the hills in the distance, and he watched their cottony shapes draw ever higher, ominously darkening the terrain. He easily traced the circuitous path up the stony bed of the mountain's torrent, along a deep ravine, curving up alongside the corn fields. His path carried him along a narrow trail winding down the far side of the village where his Mor, Afrooza Bano, and his sister, Shahr-zad, awaited his arrival in their mud-covered pucca bricked house; both women,

---

1 Mor: Pashtun word for Mother

duty-bound between those four walls, hidden away in *purdah.*

There, he was greeted by the aromatic smells of fresh *roti*[2] and chutney, the sight of his Mor smiling down at him with love in her eyes while she fanned smoke from the charred wood that kept the roti warm.

"My star has come," she said warmly.

She kissed his forehead as he sat beside her on the rugged mat against the wall. He looked lovingly at his Mor as she lightly placed another roti for him on the earthen stove. He saw the beads of her sweat shining in the light of the embers, the flush in her cheeks as she cooked for her children. He knew then, in his simple heart, that it was his most favorite sight of all. Without her existence in his life, there was nothing but an infinite void—no sky, no moon, no butterflies, nor valleys could compare. The sight of his Mor seemed to breathe life into everything, he realized, watching as she piled wood into the stove.

Those were his favorite *naan*. He never forgot the fragrant aroma of the naan his Mor cooked. Eagerly, he took one from her, but it was so hot he could barely touch it. His Mor broke it up into tiny pieces, placing a cooled morsel in his mouth.

"Eat my child, eat," she said in her lilting accent, the rhythms of her native Pashto carrying over into the Dari, every word

---

2 Roti: Bread

brimming with love.

She put some pickles with the naan in the next morsel. Touched by the warmth of Mor's hands, the mango pickle blended with the naan in his mouth, creating a mélange of tastes, one he could never quite forget. As they ate, his little sister Shahrzad sat beside him, recounting the affairs of her day; in particular, how she carried a full bucket, half her height, to the mountain stream, past the village with the other girls. She was brimming with joy to have accomplished this, to be allowed to go out of the house, even if it meant carrying weight.

It was an accepted practice that Pashtun women should remain at home, only venturing out when required for daily chores, wrapped in *chadors* and preferably in groups, or else with a male by her side—a younger brother, perhaps. There were no questions asked, no objections raised as to why women needed to be confined in this manner. Afrooza and Shahrzad followed in the long, rutted path of their mother and grandmothers and great-grandmothers in following this customary tradition with hard-minded certainty to protect their righteousness and to live in purdah, honoring the will of Allah.

Once they were done eating, Afrooza extinguished the fire in the stove, relishing in the sight of the coals dying, one after the other. Once the *cholha* had cooled down, both siblings took up one coal in their respective hands, playfully flipping them rapidly from one hand to the other to keep from being burned.

"That is enough children. Come, you're done for the day, take your sleep now," Afrooza instructed, as she tethered their gimpy old goat, as it attempted gamely to follow the kids around. "Off to sleep now, I will wait a little longer for your Baba; he went with Khan Sahib to the Jirga gathering but has not returned yet. What could it be, this late at night?" she frowned, and Bahadur heard the first, faint tone of panic in his Mor's murmuring voice. Things were not the same anymore, and there was a hidden fear lurking beneath the normality of every house in Datta Khel.

"It is no longer safe, my son," his Baba would say whenever they sat beside his grandfather's grave.

He visited the grave at least twice a week with his father, as was the custom. Graves had a special sanctity in the eyes of the Pashtuns, more even than in the case of other castes. His Baba would dismount from his horse, hold up his hands in the attitude of prayer, and invoke the blessing of God for the deceased, then stroke his beard at the conclusion of his prayer. Bahadur would copy his father in the same way and pay his blessings to his dead grandfather. Then, they would sit a while longer, enjoying the time together. Bahadur valued this time more than anything.

"Bahadur, my son," his father said during a recent visit, "visit me when I die and recite the Quran near my grave."

"Why would you talk of dying, Baba?" Bahadur was shocked and dismayed.

"And why not, my son? The fear of death follows from the fear of life. A man who lives fully is prepared to die at any time. You should never fear death. Look it in the eye when it approaches. You are my son; you are a Pashtun," he said, rolling up the sleeves of his long shirt to give water to his grandfather's grave, revealing the deep, puckered scar on his upper arm from when he was attacked during a CIA-led extortion operation, in search of Taliban militants.

Bahadur's father would always instruct him to take care of the family if something should ever happen to him. But what? He did not know exactly what it meant to die, did not understand when Baba told of the "enemy" who infiltrated their heavenly abode. He called them the "infidels." His Baba would tell him stories about the "Great War," and how the Taliban militants were trying hard to either drive them all out, kill them or recruit them.

Bahadur had heard from his friends at school that the Taliban militants were looking for young children from these neighboring areas. Some of the kids were interested because they were very poor. Not everyone had a strong Baba like him. Some of his friends spoke proudly of sacrificing in the name of false *jihad*. His Baba would get angry when he heard of this.

He would say, "If they take away the lives of our loved ones in their hunger for power, what choice is left for a peace-loving man who is left with nothing but to fight back for his family and land? Wouldn't they do the same? "His Baba clasped his hands and clenched fists with the pressure of a raging sea of anger.

Bahadur nodded incessantly to confirm both his understanding and his interest to his father. He never asked a lot of questions; afraid his father would deem him foolish. He could not make much sense out of it, but he always listened intently. He knew, even at this tender age, that his Mor would not have an idea about this "war" either; she was not privy to this or any kind of information. She had no access to television or newspapers, and even radio was scarce. Knowledge was considered a threat, so it was never invited into the house or into the lives of the women. Mor only knew that it was not safe anymore. They all heard the roar of jets and knew, from neighbors and relatives, that frequent bombings were destroying both nearby villages and crops, always thinking, always praying that their family would remain safe. Bahadur's mind was not able to comprehend the atrocities of war and the great "game of powers." However, what he did know was that he promised his Baba to take care of his family in his absence.

He took a glass of water from the modest tumbler and went

to her. "Drink some water, Mor, Baba will come, do not worry, he is very brave and strong," he professed innocently and extended the glass.

Afrooza hugged his tiny little frame. He loved the fragrance oozing out of her. Her motherly scent always traveled through the house, its invisible beauty filling the senses and proclaiming her presence, marking the territory of her nest. Afrooza Bano, the matriarch of the family, brave and honorable and diligent. Her routine was the same each day: waking before everyone else, even before the first crow of the rooster, setting in motion the rhythm of the family, like warm sunshine spilling thickly over the silent morning.

She kissed his forehead. "Yes, my star, *Inshaa Allah.* Come, it is time to sleep, you must go to Madrasah[3] tomorrow, or Maulana *sahib* will be angry with you." Her eyes had an affectionate sparkle as she spoke.

Bahadur loved going to bed, as it gave him the freedom to enjoy the peace of night, when he would count the stars with his sister from the open porch of his modest home. They would laugh and giggle, and their laughter would at times be accompanied by the roar of jets, intermittently disrupting the quiet harmony. Still, it was the best time, he thought, in his beautiful village, a place

---

3 Madrasah: School

where he played games with his sibling and friends, attending festivals and ceremonies, basking in the love and goodness of his home, amidst the folk songs and stories and the dance and dhole. Bahadur had already gone to his bed, but he was anything but sleepy, he was just about to count the stars when there came a heavy knock on the door. His Baba came in out of the cold and darkness, letting in a gust of icy wind. The light of his lantern revealed the graceful geometric designs his children had daubed on the walls with the red earth of the mountains. After dinner, Afrooza sat next to her husband, adjusting her veil over shiny dark braids, and poured him another glass of tea. Bahadur was under the blanket, listening intently to their conversation. "The kids are asleep?" he inquired. Afrooza nodded, silently. ""Things are not looking good Bano, we are living in the middle of drone strikes, army assaults, Kalashnikovs, and suicide attacks from the Taliban. And now, the government is demolishing our houses, pushing us to the edge of Bannu. Our tribe is forced to leave behind all of our belongings—our homes, cattle, fields, businesses, and properties, including our shops in the bazaars of Mirali and Minashah." Zaram's face seemed shadowy as he worriedly looked at his children. Afrooza just kept listening, in silence, as Zaram continued to speak.

"I know this does not make much sense to you, but I am

sharing this because the Jirga decided we should relocate to safer places, for the sake of keeping our women and children safe and away from harm."

"But, where will we go, Khan?" Afrooza finally said, anxiously. Zaram hurriedly stood up, while stroking his beard, he retorted. "Keep everything ready, the convoy will set off tomorrow night after dark. Safdar Khan and his men will take us across the border to a safe house near Landi Kotal, inside Pakistan's Khyber Tribal Agency." Afrooza kept looking at him, keeping her hands folded in her lap so he wouldn't see how nervous she was at the idea of migration.

"Do not worry, Banu," Zaram said, assuredly. "The Jirga families are going too. Once I know that you and the kids are safe, I will come back and fight alongside other men from our tribe, for I cannot simply sit and watch my paradise rot away. These militants have sold their souls and loyalty for the American dollar, my blood boils when I see them commit such horrendous crimes, toward us; we are from the same faith, we have the same blood in our veins, but they have traded theirs for weapons and power. I spit on their treachery, and I won't rest unless I liberate my land from these infidels and traitors. I owe it to my people and this soil."

"How many will you fight Khan? And for how long? The

other women tell me there are an endless number of militants, who want to drive us all out and abduct our children, how many? "Afrooza asked, blankly staring at her husband.

"All of them, I will fight all, until my last breath!" Zaram could not say more, he clenched his fist, fixed his toque, and went out to kiss Bahadur and Shahr who were lying down peacefully in the veranda, under the moonlit sky, free of all worries and the brisk bitterness of reality. Bahadur who was playacting at sleep felt his Baba's eyes on his face. His Baba looked intently at their little faces and the stress oozing out of his time creased leathery forehead started to escape and soon was replaced with a paternal smile bracing his lips. He knew he was doing the right thing for his children and family.

But Afrooza knew that it would be she and her kids who would miss their modest brick house the most. They would miss the stirred activity in the dark cool rooms that smelled of the damp earth, walking from one end to the other.

The next week found the quiet moments of their Friday morning, punctuated by the crackling bass growl of the drones reverberating and shaking the whole house before receding into the distance. No one in the household paid attention; they'd grown used to the sounds of war—they'd grown up with it. Afrooza was the first to wake. She knew her kids would be follow soon, while Zaram would slumber on till the breakfast was made and the house was clean and tidy. She dunked her hands in the bucket of cool mountain water and let big silver drops rain down with quick flicks of her fingertips. Once the ground was damp and softened, she swept and tamped it down, releasing a sweet earthy fragrance. She knew she would miss the scent terribly, after today, and the thought made her eyes well with tears.

The enticing fragrance of breakfast woke Bahadur and Shahrzad, as smells of fresh potatoes and chopped mint, mixed with the aromatic *Naan* bread and black tea tantalized their appetites. Bahadur rubbed his eyes and got up, and after washing his face in the nearby basin, went and sat next to his mother in the kitchen, the heart of their home.

Afrooza was busy making fresh lassi for Zaram, made by churning fresh goat milk inside a barrel. She raised her head and spoke affectionately.

"Bahadur, my star, you've awoken. Would you do your mother a favor, please? Would you go to the stream and bring me another bucket of water?"

Bahadur gladly took the bucket from her. As he was walking out, he heard his mother showering innumerable blessings on him. He walked with the bucket, nearly half his height, to the nearby brook that wandered past his village in a silver thread, bubbling with fresh, cold water. The rippling water tempted him, and he jumped in, where lotus-like flowers adorned the surface, floating like fragile teacups. As he surfaced, he heard a growling rumble like thunder from the direction of his house, getting louder and louder by the second. From over the brook, just beneath the cloud base, he saw a black dot, hurtling towards the direction of his house and getting bigger moment by moment. His little heart skipped a beat and he dashed out of the water and turned back the way he'd come, making sure to fill the water bucket for fear of disappointing his mother.

By the time Bahadur arrived back, the heavy bucket spilling over, in a shrieking, deafening, earsplitting crescendo that completely overwhelmed the chorus of his fast-beating heart, a missile fired by the drone tore through his pucca brick house, leaving behind nothing but black smoke and flames. He broke out in a cold sweat, shaking from thc inside out, choked, and dizzy, not able to speak or move; a glazed stare of terror etched on his face. He was blinking through layers of smoke at his loss and he stared for some moments without understanding. The tilt of the space where he was standing had a deep, innate wrongness. There was a strong sense of being alone, in wintry deadness. Nothing made sense in any direction. He squinted his eyes nearly shut to pretend that nothing was wrong, but the jabs of pain reassured him that he was awake and that this wasn't just one long, horrible nightmare. "Mor…" he managed to utter as his eyes fluttered open and the bucket fell from his hands.

Bahadur ran, breathlessly and fanatically toward the debris, his eyes welling over with tears. He dug desperately, hysterically, seeking for a glimpse of his family, to embrace his mother one last time, to feel the touch of his father's hand on his head, one last time, to pull his little sister's braid, one last time. Please, please, just one time, just one time . . . His heart pleaded while his small hands dug deep into the mud. His jaw hurt; his face and knees were cut; his mouth was like sandpaper. Blinking uncomprehendingly at the chaos, he grappled around in the wreckage – upending dusty shreds of tattered clothes, snatching his hands back at hot things and shards of broken belongings, more and more troubled by the way the rubble gave under his feet in spots, and by the soft, inert lumps at the edge of his tear-stained vision. For hours, he plowed, sobbing, unwilling to believe it could all be taken in a moment. He desperately dug through the ruins looking for his family, calling their names out again and again. No answer.

"Mor!" Bahadur screamed in agony as his bloodied and battered hands touched a tattered piece of his mother's black chador in the mess of wood and brick rubble. He dug some more, in hopes to find a glimpse of her, perhaps she is alive.

Nothing.

Nothing. Bahadur's eyes showed such depths of pain and sorrow as he remembered how she encircled him in her warm and comforting chador, her arms around him. And how much he loved the appealing maternal scent that oozed out of her clothes, calming his nerves, and giving him a feeling of safety and protection.

He would never feel safe again. Bahadur gripped the remaining piece of her chador so hard that his knuckles turned white. He held it next to his heart, rubbing it to hold onto his mother's love. His tears made wet tracks down his face only to melt into the piece of cloth.

The pain of recognizing all he had just lost, pulsating through his ten-year-old mind so intensely that he collapsed onto the debris that he once called *home.*

THE ABYSS

That Friday morning, around 5:30 a.m. the townsfolk of Datta Khel heard three successive explosions. The noise grew louder by the second. Amidst the smoldering remains of their homes, the people of the town sifted through the debris in desperation hoping against hope to save their families.

After less than an hour of hell, while the people of the town were still hopelessly embroiled in the blazing havoc, no one paid much attention to young Bahadur making his way, stumbling, staggering off the piles of rubble. His expression was flat, his skin paper-thin, and his eyes distended, blood-red and desiccated from rubbing at them. His walk was seethed with anxiety and fear as he dragged along his dust-strewn rucksack, under a quiet and musty opalescent sky that streamed with sunlight, shimmering in tilted columns of dust motes. Beads of sweat coagulated his innocent face. His eyes were bloodshot and swollen, empty and tired, and showed dark purple circles beneath. His cheeks were hollow, and tearstained. His bottom lip was bright red and chapped with tiny cuts and dried blood from biting at it, the upper lip almost as white as his face. Pale as a ghost child, he continued, lost in time.

He passed by the nearby mosque, a sight of ruin and destruction, stopping for a moment to gaze up at the deserted alley. This mosque used to be his *madrasah*. He would come here for recitation with his father, for classes on religious teachings. Now, it presented a stark reminder of what was gone. These streets, where his uncles sat with their neighbors, chatting, cracking jokes and sipping tea with his father, while he stood nearby, bored, and restless, thinking about when he could go to the nearby playground where he and the other village kids played cricket and football together. It was here that he had first heard about drones. He was 7 years old, sitting in his school classroom in eastern Waziristan. A group of his friends animatedly discussed the recent death of a local man.

"Then the drone came," one of them said, imitating the whistling noise of an unmanned aircraft, "and he was dead."

Bahadur didn't understand what they were saying. It was as if he was the only one left out of a secret. He finally decided to ask his teacher, "What did the other boys mean? What was a drone?"

The teacher's response was both ominous and prescient. "It's something that, once you come to its attention, you will not be left to live," he told Bahadur.

That was three years ago. Since then, his father had said that their province was now a hub for armed groups—and a bustling drug trade. He had said it had become one of the most drone-bombed provinces in the world. They should move. Even then, his ten-year-old mind could never have imagined that a drone would take everything away from him, in a split second; he stood there, lost in the precariousness of his childhood, where the boundaries of his innocence and reality were disturbingly melded. He thought about his Mor. Thought about Baba. Thought about Shahr. His pucca brick house until a dull distant purr of a drone that within moments swelled into a rattling sound uncoiled his adverse fate and brought him back to reality. He gave only an empty, fleeting glance at the inscription: *Praise only be to Allah.* Unconsciously, he bit at his lower lip and continued when he heard a familiar voice. It was Maulana sahib, his madrasah teacher. Bahadur would go to the madrasah every evening to learn the recitation of the Quran from him. He was the local cleric in the mosque, and in reverence, everyone called him Maulana, the religious scholar of the local community. Probably in his late fifties or early sixties, he was a short man with a four-inch black beard and wore a pale white shalwar kameez with the physique of an oak tree.

"Bahadur? *Bacha*[4], where are you going? Haven't you heard the buzzing noise and the loud blast, thereafter? *Astagfirullah*! No one is willing to come out and look where it hit, as it is still not safe. You should be indoors with your mother and sister, just like the rest. What are you carrying behind you in the sack?

He looked disenchanted. Maulana could not hold his gaze but for a moment, for Bahadur's stare carried a sea of sadness that could submerge the whole world inside it, and still not allay even an inch of his pain. Trying to escape the disturbing moment, Maulana came forward and peered into the sack; inside, he saw nothing but heaps of moist red sand.

"What is this, Bacha?" Maulana asked curiously.

"This is what remains of my family, after that thing fell out of the sky," came his muted response. "I could not find anything else in the rubble, except for this." He blankly pointed at the shredded piece of his mother's chador that he had tied around his finger. "I dug for hours to find my Mor, my Baba and Shahr, but they have disappeared into the sand. And so, I am carrying some to bury in the graveyard."

---

4 Bacha: child

The echoes of war sounded again momentarily in the distance. Bahadur was not even stirred by his newest considerations: how would he, a ten-year-old child, shoulder the burden of his loss alone? He was numb, disoriented and beyond consolation. He did not ask for an embrace, not a sob or tear came out of his eyes. For now, he was more concerned about holding on to whatever shreds of his old life lingered, of his family, now dead.

But Maulana knew, his conniving mind instantly identifying yet another lost childhood among so many others he'd seen and exploited. A childhood spent negotiating such an intolerant landscape without obtaining permanent scars was an impossible feat; now, Bahadur's life was a living hell. He looked over the boy's permanently scarred hands, their broken nails crusted with dried blood, his bloodshot eyes and blank stare, and he knew exactly what was left to claim.

The possibility of gaining profit from this enterprising opportunity excited him. Just as a heavy dusk deepened over the craggy hills, a muezzin's voice called the faithful to prayer, piercing the jarring noise of drones. Bahadur remembered how once the mosque was filled with the sound of scraping benches, clinking footsteps, and the rustle of clothing as men knelt and made obeisance to Allah. Now, the mosque is half-stood with dilapidated silent pillars, lone and grey. "Come, my son, let us go inside and pray first. I will bury this with you, don't worry at all. You are not alone, you are in Allah's refuge now," Maulana said with conniving kindness, taking up Bahadur's tiny frame in his arms and inside the ruined mosque.

Though the back wall gaped open, and half the floor was missing, the mosque was still sacred, and someone had strewn fresh straw on the floor. In the shadow of carved wooden columns, there were a few men turned away from the destruction behind them, facing the niche that marked the direction of Mecca as they prayed, their weapons laid before them.

Maulana spread his *pattu* on the ground, then stood and bowed and stood again. In the silence, Bahadur stood behind him, following along thoughtlessly. When they'd finished praying, Maulana introduced him to the other men in the room, explaining what had happened to the boy.

"Everything was destroyed after the drone attack," he said. "Everything inside the house, buried under the earth, his family . . . buried under the earth." Maulana turned and whispered to one of the men, Hakeem Shah, who had a broad and meaty face, a strong, prominent nose, and full lips. His untrimmed beard was gray at the temples and ran in milky streaks below his chin. On his high forehead, framed by the swaths of his turban, was a darkened callus formed by many hours of prayerful prostration.

His eyes reflected the sort of decisiveness one might expect in a medical man, but they also showed a measure of serenity that seemed oddly out of place.

"He is only a poor orphan now—just the way you prefer."

Hakeem and Maulana took Bahadur to the nearby graveyard, where they buried the remains of the blood-stained silt to appease the little boy's heart. Once they were done reciting *Fateha*[5], Maulana rubbed his hand on Bahadur's head and asked cleverly, "Do you want to see your Amma, Baba, and little sister again, Bahadur? Do you want to be with them again?" The boy nodded and looked up with eager hope.

"Well, there is surely a way, Bacha. If you make God happy, he will unite you with your family again in the heavens above," he cajoled.

"How can I make God happy?" little Bahadur asked, tugging on Maulana's finger. "I want to be with my Amma, I miss her so much."

"By doing God's work, by becoming his soldier and devoting your life fully to his mission. Hakeem will take care of you. He will raise you into a brave lion, like his very own, will feed you and look after you, if you do as he says. Today marks the birth of a new Bahadur—the righteous one."

---

5 Fateha: First Koranic verse in the Holy book of Muslims

He then fastened an amulet around Bahadur's neck, one containing Koranic verses. "This will help you survive," he said reassuringly. "God will help you endure the fire. You will be saved, and you will meet your Mor and Baba and little sister in paradise." Maulana lifted the amulet away from around Bahadur's neck as if to confirm his promise.

The sun was nearly to the edge of the sharp, mountainous peaks and ridges that marked the far limits of the valley as Hakeem pointed to a cluster of nondescript mud buildings on a hilltop about a kilometer away. "That is our check post for now, until we move out to Mir Ali, in the East. Every night, the mujahidin or the army attack this post. We are always surrounded by death, by a rain of bullets. Are you ready to go with us to fulfill your destiny? My men are waiting for you."

It was not a polite question, but an order. With hopes of seeing his family again, Bahadur couldn't say anything but yes. Maulana came forward with a bottle of water and helped Bahadur perform his ablutions. "Now then, Bacha, you are cleansed. In God's name, recite the *kalma*."

THE UNEARTHLY RETROGRADE

Bahadur had been instructed to always keep himself clean, to perform his ablutions five times a day. The only color he was allowed to wear was white, as it denoted God's holy warriors. In the religious military camp, he learned to "listen and obey." The masters made all the children declare, "I must listen and obey even if I have to die." And though everything about the camp was based on a systematic code created to indoctrinate children to hate and grave discrimination, everything that was said and taught was declared to be the word of God. Bahadur and his family regularly attended the mosque, and his father sometimes led the call to prayer. He knew somewhat in his innocent mind that these teachings were not reflective of what his father used to say. However, as a seven-year-old, he was not able to fully judge between them at the very beginning of his indoctrination, so he just went with the evidence available via the pulpit, as he could not know when people were lying.

Bahadur was placed with a group of new recruits, aged six to eleven, completely isolated from the rest, led by a man known as Master Qari. Feared and admired by all, his black eyes shone like two polished gems upon his tanned face, partially obscured behind thick brows. His hands were pale, long, and gentle, moving gracefully as he spoke, as though mapping the course of a soaring bird. His chin and cheeks were covered by a thick grey beard, and when he smiled his teeth flashed from between crimson lips, white as freshly fallen snow. His clothing, different from the rest of the black turbans, was of an Eastern cut: a long robe, colored a dull red, the color of freshly dried blood, topped by a green turban wound around his head. Only men of very high and noble rank were allowed to wear Eastern cut robes and colors as their stately dress accentuated their nobler rank and solemn mien. He was always reciting something, silently counting the beads of the *tesbih*[6], twined around his fingers. Right away, it was clear he held a special place in the camp. He was the religious

---

6 Tesbih: rosary

ecclesiastic, the Maulana of the group, the master of psychological indoctrination, and revered by all.

The training facility was in the remote area of Nawazkot in South Waziristan. It was an abandoned school where Bahadur and the rest of the children were kept. The adult trainees were segregated from the minors and kept in separate facilities. The government had little oversight or control, which reduced the need for camp security. At night, however, a senior trainee guarded the camp, and no one was allowed to leave the camp after night prayers. Each day, as early as four in the morning, the kids would gather on the floor of the training encampment room, rocking back and forth, memorizing the Koran. The chamber was huge in size and looked as though it might once have been some holy mosque, so monumentally solemn were its proportions, so sober and mellowed its white stone walls. Most of it was enveloped in profoundest shadow, but the inquisitive sun rays were penetrating always farther through the doors, gradually revealing the miscellaneous agglomeration of audio recordings, video tapes and numerous distorted references from the scripture.

They were not allowed to ask questions. Bahadur, along with the other children, had brought a basic understanding already of the fundamentals of their faith. This, however, was quickly and subtly corrupted and replaced with the fanatic jingoism of extremism. Convincing young children to sacrifice their lives without question required intensive indoctrination. The tool of fear was actively used to condition the children. They were forced to chew the delusion, or they could suffer the wrath of God and their masters.

Master Qari would begin his fiery unending rhetoric, laced with distorted interpretations, preaching to the young recruits, most of them kidnapped from refugee camps, recruited from madrassas, schools or mosques, or simply sold off by their impoverished families in exchange for clothing, food, and shelter. These boys were considered especially valuable to the terrorist groups, as they were unsullied, easily influenced, and less likely to be caught. Most of them were easily convinced, given their youth, and their lessons were devised to reinforce the objectives of the terrorists. And, as with most religious teachings, the fierier the rhetoric, the greater the impact on their young minds.

Their day began with Master Qari feeding them the anti-western tirades that he read from a well-planned script. "My children, your religion is the most superior in the universe; yours is the only true religion. All the rest are false, erroneous; the adherents of those other religions are a barrier to the growth of the one *true* religion. You are the chosen ones, the ones to which Allah has bequeathed his da'wa[7], bequeathed himself. You are here to do his work, to wage war against the infidels who destroy your homes, who kill your families, who tarnish your faith. You have been commanded to fight against these disbelievers, to wage holy jihad until they relent, testify, and yield to us! In reward, you will not be harmed! Allah will protect you and keep you safe. And if you sacrifice yourselves to his path, heaven and its untold pleasures will be your reward for death in the cause of Allah. There, you will be reunited with your family, live in a castle, drink from cool streams of milk; there, you will dress in the finest silk and enjoy the finest food. Whatever your heart desires, thus will be gifted upon you. Such is the power of your lord. Indeed, his reward is the greatest of all. Do you want to be a miserable sinner? Or Allah's warrior?"

"Allah's warrior!" they all cried in a single voice, oblivious to what was truly meant by Master Qari's words.

"Shabashay[8]! Repeat after me! Allah ho Akbar—Praise be to God!". They all repeated that same rocking motion chanting hateful slogans.

Bahadur was unsure of himself, so he mimicked everyone's actions, he was nervous and scared. He just repeated all the recitations and lengthy proclamations, again and again, a growing

---

7 Da'wa: invite

8 Shabashay: Well-Done

chant, driving the ideals deep into their minds as they repeated over and over, like a stuck needle on a record player.

They were taught how to pray, how to recite, how to surrender to Allah's will; and, most especially, how to hate the enemy. There was no playtime, no space for imagination, sports, or entertainment. No television or outdoor play was allowed. Any joking, laughter, or friendship was a punishable act. As such, they were not even allowed to know each other. There were no women in the camp, and so quickly the ideas of affection and physical expressions of love became unfamiliar. The only sweet talk came from Master Qari.

Still, Bahadur smelled the fear and hate behind the man's sweet, lilting voice. He was perceptive for his age, intelligent enough that he might have had a bright future, had he been anywhere else. Bahadur eventually learned to hide his anger and fear. His eyes slowly got empty, and he started to feel nothing. Reactivating emotion meant facing grief over his lost family, guilt over seeing his friends getting tortured and sexually harassed or whatever else he was expected to do, to remain alive. So, he stayed numb and followed orders.

The children followed a strict routine. The only reading or writing they were exposed to was fundamentally religious. They were given nourishment enough to keep them fit and healthy and took frequent breaks for rest. Small doses of the drug Pervitin were mixed in the food to numb their senses, and gradually impede their ability to distinguish right from wrong. The drug, while still allowing them to remain active, held their minds in a dull stupor. And the only persistent voice they ever heard was that of Master Qari.

Even though Bahadur had learned to play along in showcasing allegiance, he longed to return to the solace of his mountain paradise, to run with his sheep and spiral-horned cattle. But it was not safe anymore, and so there was nowhere to run. Fear stalked him, lurking around every corner. Fighting echoed across the hills, as though the whole world was under attack. He was stuck right where he was, between the vastness of the desert and the looming mountains of Hindu Kush.

As he grew older, he understood the price of freedom when one of his campmates was crucified for disobeying the masters' dictates, a punishment he had seen happen almost weekly. The dead were left rotting for days out in the open, wearing a sign describing their crime — usually refusal to convert or trying to escape. Seeing his friend die in front of his eyes, made Bahadur rebellious. The lectures were not enough to stop the nightmares or flashbacks or to purge the guilt he felt, which channeled inward into depression and outward to rage. He knew there was no way out, so he became defiant in his own way, pushing back where he could, missing his prayers, or refusing to eat the food that made him feel dull and stupid. As he spent more time there, he grew more and more insubordinate as he sometimes refused to see the slaughtering videos or give in to the idea of killing. Somewhere, in his subconscious mind, the teachings of his father still held more substance than the perverse reality he was forced to receive.

Once, he stood up to defend another one of his friends who got strung up and tortured for not listening or obeying the commands.

"I will not let you hurt him!" Bahadur had jumped in front of Mustafa, his friend with a surge of adrenaline fueling a fast-beating heart, stroking his emotion of hate, driving his anger higher. The price of his defiance was nothing but pain. As expected, this drew the wrath of the masters as Bahadur's legs and hands were tied and he was lashed or beaten brutally as punishment. He expected death each day, and yet continued to live, much to his disappointment. After several months with Master Qari, the recruits were introduced to their most important tool, the implement used to launch them toward their multitude of gifts in heaven—*the suicide jacket.*

By now, the boys were taking their lectures in a different room. Most of the walls were curiously colourless: all their tints were toned off, dull, dead, or faded, giving them a weird, gloomy appearance, as though a breath of corruption had passed over them, blighting them, paling them, filling them with a ghastly secretive light that held unexplained mysteries, dreadful undiscovered possibilities, awaiting to be called forth to real life. This time, the training was with a different face, a turban named Bhaitani. With painstaking thoroughness, the children were taught all about the suicide jacket, starting from the trigger mechanism, through to its contents and effects. A magical thing, whose detonation would transport them directly to the heavens above, but only if they first removed Master Qari's gifted talisman containing religious verses— wearing the talisman would protect them from the explosion and kill only the enemy. They were also instructed to look down while pulling the handle on the suicide jacket. This ensured that their faces were obliterated, and the infidels unable to identify them, or the training camp from which they'd come, improving the others' chances of ascension to heaven. Or, as Bhaitani would say, "A win-win for Allah's holy warriors, *Alhamdulillah—God is great*!"

In the evenings, additional indoctrination classes were conducted, taking the psychological brainwashing to a deeper level. Master Qari ran these lectures with fanaticism and aggression, employing both visual and audio stimuli: sets of images flashed quickly before the children's eyes, interrupting their ability to process them; at the same time, sounds were played either below the range of hearing, or overloud. Masked sounds, sounds played backward, all of it meant to implant subliminal thoughts of destruction, death, and mayhem into the minds of the children. Anyone who covered their eyes or ears were whipped viciously.

"My children, you must stay away from all manner of worldly pleasures. Modernity and the secular culture of the West are abominable sins. The import of Western culture, along with their educational system, is leading the faithful away from Allah. The disbelief of the West is so grave a sin as to merit death. A hurdle to the spread of our one true faith. It drives your women out of purdah in the name of freedom! Arrogantly they show off their bodies, driving cars, going to schools for their *modern* education. *Astagfirullah! Astagfirullah—May Allah forgive us*!"

Then, the entire room would echo the master's words including Bahadur as the hatred now fully consumed his eleven-year-old mind.

Master Qari would then put up a set of images on the projector screen, showing incursions, gory images of war, mutilated bodies amidst the piercing wailing of Muslim women and children, filling the recruits with a blinding rage.

Bhaitani would begin to aggressively chant "Allah is humiliating us! Allah is humiliating the Muslims in Syria, Iraq, Palestine, and Waziristan, Afghanistan—everywhere! Our brethren have strayed from the path of God; and that is why He has made the infidel, sin-loving people masters of the entire planet. But we, as his holy warriors, will not sit quietly and let the enemy destroy us. We will fight! We and our brothers from all over the world will wage jihad, killing each one of them until they yield!" The deafening sound of *Allah ho Akbar* would then be heard across the campsite, Bahadur's roar sounding along with the rest.

The last phase of Bahadur's proselytization was based on the subliminal stimuli. Master Qari called it *below the threshold* indoctrination. Bahadur and the rest of the children were taken to a special hall inside the facility. Unlike previously, when the only rooms they were kept in were plain and white, this one had a completely different feel to it. Instead, its walls were painted with beautiful images of lush green vistas, dotted with fruit-laden trees separated by streams of milk and honey. Images of beautiful women beamed from the walls, inviting smiles from the viewer. After spending several months within the confines of white walls and bland parapets, the scene was dreamlike, overwhelming Bahadur's mind. The other children had similar reactions, impatient now to sacrifice themselves, and be transported to this place, into Allah's abode.

It was then that Master Qari came back to them, a broad smile on his face, accompanied by the *Amir*, Hakeem Shah. His voice echoed in the hall, "My dear children, your training is over, and you must now await your calling. Remember! Do not feel guilty for the victims. Sometimes, while killing the enemy, you must kill the innocent as well. But do not fear, you will carry them to the heavens with you. They will be waiting at the gates of heaven to greet you with chaplets and crowns. May Allah's help be with you!"

The cycles of these fundamentalist lectures continued for months and years. New recruits would come and go at the bidding of the extremist leaders. Some would survive the attacks and return; many did not. Those who did return continued in their training and were given practical drills on the use of weapons. During Bahadur's ideological training, there were no guns or military-style training; eventually, as the years passed and he turned seventeen, he was exposed to the entire armory. Bahadur, being a curious mind, always wondered about the means and the money to buy such high-tech weaponry. Finally, one night, while passing by their camp, he overheard Hakeem speaking with one of his commanders, Khanan, of billions of dollars and stockpiles of guns. "We are not taking it from the people, we are taking it from our enemy. After all, we are working *for* them, not against them. All that we have amounts to what they spend in ten days to defeat us. Can you imagine?" At this, both men began to laugh uncontrollably.

It was two o'clock in the morning, and Bahadur could not sleep, so he had left his bed to take the air, which he often did, even though it was not allowed. But he had no fear of the consequences as he had already lost the will to live.

Hakeem's shelter was away from the rest, and heavily guarded. None of the recruits were allowed to come near his camp. But tonight, surprisingly, the guards had fallen asleep. It was the beginning of December, when the desert became cold at night. The fire the guards huddled around still burned brightly, and Bahadur heard their snoring in the dark.

Moving closer, he heard Hakeem's voice rising out from his room, engaged in light banter. Bahadur had never heard Hakeem laugh like that before, and crept forward, his tautly muscled frame leaning towards the door. When he peered into the room, the smell of hashish and booze touched his nostrils. He saw Hakeem Shah sitting in the center with two other men. One was commander Khanan, but the other was hidden in the shadows, his back facing the door.

"Yes! First, it was Al Qaeda—but who can tell me the name of their father? Who?"

Hakeem stood up, swaying happily while the other two guffawed. "Tell us—tell us, Shah!"

"I will tell you! I was there, from the moment of baptism,

up until the end. Lest you forget, the CIA gave birth to us. Ah, I remember each second of it. It runs in my blood like poison," Hakeem heard his own voice echoing, returning him back to his childhood. And he had a momentary glimpse of a memory, long forgotten.

At any moment, Hakeem had thought in those days, he too would look up and his father would be there, waiting for him. He did not know that everything would change in a spin of a moment and his world would come crashing down around him and he would be headed into a landscape that was a maze of shattered dreams and bright futures.

Hakeem's father Ahmed Abdullah, a noble Pashtun, was an austere Muslim. He kept faith with his traditions and submitted to an arranged marriage with a second cousin, as was the tribal custom. Abdullah had two boys and four girls with Hakeem's mother Arezo staying at home, following tradition. Born in 1960, Hakeem was the oldest son. He attended the nearby government Daqeeq Islamia School, where most of the subjects were Islamic. Hakeem loved reciting the Quran, it was his favorite subject even though his father did not know how to recite. Even since his childhood, he saw his father with guns and men with big beards. His father's Kalashnikov was always hidden in a wood pile by the door. His father would often take it out, clean it, oiled rags on its parts, and the smell of gunmetal would make him feel "safe." Hakeem never liked his father's shouting, it was like the hot dust wind from the desert, and he was never sure when it would strike him and his other siblings. His mother had gotten used to his father's short temper, as following the customs, women were submissive and obedient to their husbands. But she would always defend her children when it came to their safety.

"Leave him alone, Abu Hakeem," his mother always said to his father. Farida, Hakeem's beloved mother, considered Hakeem to be Allah's blessing, as her first born. She loved him, more than herself. That is why she would call herself and her husband from the *kunya*, "father and mother of Hakeem" She always took Hakeem's side, even in case of her other children, which further provoked Ahmed as he could see Hakeem getting spoiled. If their fight got too bad, Hakeem would flee to his Grandparents' house, which was situated just a few yards away. His Grandparents always welcomed him with kisses, surrounding him in their old smell of sandal-wood oil. Once a month, his mother would count out his father's earnings from fighting in the mountains or farming. She would then send him and his younger brother Omar, to the large bazaar in Qala-i-Zal, where the vendors sold everything, from spices to fine cooking oils, candles, and clothing and for children, kites, and handmade wooden toys. Among the crowded stalls of the bazaar, Hakeem would go directly to the kite shop and buy himself and his brother kites to fly, once their father went out for his work, for days and sometimes, weeks. Ahmed was very strict when it came to his boys' hobbies and interests. He couldn't care less for his daughters as their destiny was already defined by the Pashtun tradition. He just wanted his boys to go to madrassah.

When they returned home, Hakeem's mother would hide the boys' kites behind the birch wood cradle where she'd rocked his youngest sister Bano.

Their mud-walled house was small, two- thatched roofed rooms with a patio between them. The secret of flying kites made Hakeem feel close to his mother and brother. Hakeem shared a different relationship with his father, it was more of authority and respect. He looked up to him. When Hakeem turned thirteen, Ahmed started taking him and his twelve-year-old brother Omar to the farm. Like most men of their tribe, his father had farmed a small plot. He taught his sons how to irrigate a field with water, and how to place a boulder at the curve of the furrow to avoid erosion. He taught these lessons to his sons, as they grew old, working by his side, the soil binding them together, sure as blood.

By the time Hakeem turned sixteen, he had turned six feet tall, but was thin as a date pit. But that did not stop his father from taking him to the mountains for training. Ahmed's group operated under the Haqqanis but later shifted to the Hezb-e-Islami. When Ahmed was killed a year before the Afghan-Soviet War, his group had again joined the Haqqanis, but they were now serving the Taliban.

It was a bright sunny morning when Ahmed had returned home from the Jirga meeting. Sun from the open roof warmed Ahmed's face as he looked around, holding eye contact with Hakeem, then his mother with disapproval in his eyes. "How many times do I have to repeat myself in this house, Farida, Hakeem is as big as an oak tree now, he should neither sit and eat with the women, nor sleep in the same room!"

"I like to keep him with me, Ahmed, he is the apple of my eyes." Farida caressed Hakeem's hair, affectionately who was eating alongside his mother. Ahmed grabbed Hakeem from the collar and pushed him away from the eating mat. "You are making my son characterless; you, foolish woman! A boy who hides behind his mother's chador will not stand up to anything. Listen carefully, Hakeem!" Ahmed grabbed Hakeem from both shoulders and looked directly at him, "If I see you with your mother again, for eating or sleeping, I will beat the life out of you! You are the man of the house, son, act according to your customs. Omar will follow in your footsteps. Set a manly example. Farida!" Hakeem's authoritative voice echoed in the veranda. "Where is Hakeem's *shemagh*! Bring it here, right now!" Farida ran inside and hurriedly brought a piece of fine cotton cloth, used for the headdress. She obediently handed it over to Ahmed. "There! Now, you look like a true Pashtun, do not take this off. This represents our tribal identity; our honor and it will serve as a reminder that you are a military commander's eldest son." Ahmed's voice was full of pride as he settled the *shemag* on Hakeem's head. And Hakeem obeyed his father and never did take it off, after his command. He loved his father dearly and did not want to disappoint him.

When he last saw his father and mother, it was the summer of 1979. Ahmed had come home early this season as he and his tribe had disobeyed Hezb-e-Islami's commands of tax extortion in the nearby village. It was a sunny Sunday morning when Hakeem had gone out with his brother Omar to gather pine nuts from the trees. They wandered away from their home, towards the tall trees lining a ridge. Hakeem was taller than Omar, so he climbed the thick trunk and started to shake the branches. Omar gathered the cones that fell, cracking them open and picking their nuts.

"Look, Omar! Look, how fast I can climb." Hakeem had grown strong enough to climb onto the tallest branches. His arms would grasp above him as he took strong assured steps up the tree.

"Bravo, brother! You really are strong and fast. I wish I could do that, too." Omar clapped with childlike excitement.

"I could have taught you, but soon, you will not be spending time with me, Omar, will you miss me, when baba sends you off to Taloqan, huh?" Hakeem asked, his head tilted back, staring up at his younger brother among the pine branches. Ahmed was planning on sending Omar to a bigger madrassah in Taloqan as he was the first to learn Quran by heart while Hakeem's interest had diverted away from studies, to farming and fighting alongside his father.

"Soon, you will not be spending time with me, Omar, will you miss me?" Hakeem asked, his head tilted back, staring up at his younger brother among the pine branches.

"I sure will, brother. I am leaving this summer and I am already nervous." Omar said.

"Do not worry, Omar. You will see me when you come to the mountains in two years, when you are old enough to fight, you will join me and father."

Omar's pockets were nearly filled with nuts when they heard jeeps approaching. Omar climbed onto the branches with Hakeem. They both saw a dust of people running. Behind the dust were jeeps, loaded with men with guns who looked like their father, going towards their village. They shot the villagers as they ran, including children. Hakeem's blood boiled as he saw the scene, he tried climbing down but Omar held onto his arm. They both hid among the branches. Hakeem consoled Omar, who was weeping bitterly.

"Do not fear, little brother, Baba has a Kalashnikov too, remember? And these men know him!" Soon the sound of shooting finished. Hakeem and Omar could see smoke, erupting from flames. The men lit the thatched roofs of their homes on fire. Still, Hakeem told Omar not to worry as Baba had a gun and no harm could come to him and his mother and sisters.

All that day, the fire burned the houses. The wind choked them from the smoke coming from their village. They had no food or water. Devastated and scared, they returned to their village in the morning. The jeeps and the men with beards and guns were gone. Kunduz was smoldering and burning. There was little or nothing left of their home. The carpets were little more than ash brushed across a dirt floor. The cradle had collapsed into a pile of scorched sticks. All that remained was the charred pieces of their mother's chador which she might have used to drape their sisters, to save them from the fire. And the scalded remains of their father's turban. But their father's Kalashnikov remained hidden by the door, mixed with the woodpile embers. Hakeem reached for the gun, with trembling hands and blood red eyes while Omar clutched his hand to his chest to contain the string of pain and tremor.

"This is no longer home, Omar. Let us go." Hakeem's blank voice jarred in the silence of death and misery. Omar opened his mouth to speak but his throat was choked with the sorrow of all he'd lost. He swallowed and asked. "Where to, brother?"

"To the mountains." Hakeem answered, staring in blank space, as if he was already there. Omar felt as if Hakeem had grown into a man, in just a day. He nodded and was fully ready to follow his brother's command. Hakeem's father taught him about *badal*, revenge. He used to instruct him that it was Hakeem's duty as a Pashtun to take revenge when his honor was at stake. As they went up the mountains to pledge their loyalties to the Haqqani militants, their strange glares made Hakeem ache for a time when he would be ready and big enough to take badal against those who killed his family.

The Haqqanis knew that Ahmed, their father, and entire family was killed by the Hezb-e-Islami militia. The Haqqani warlords saw great potential in Hakeem and Omar's grief-stricken rage as they were not only the sons of a great military commander but were also seething in the desire for revenge. The seeds of hatred were already planted, now was the time to carefully support its growth into a firmly rooted tree.

"Why should we listen to them, brother? They are asking us to kill innocent people," Omar would ask, grossly surveying their surroundings.

"Because being part of this armed group means having a haven and food to eat and do not forget, we must avenge our father and mother. This is the only way to do it." Hakeem knew that they had come too far now to go back. Winter was looming and their survival depended on staying in this camp and complying with the will of the commanders.

When Hakeem opened his eyes in the morning, he could barely breathe. He freed himself from the blanket and clawed at his face. Ice had frozen on his face and mouth. He tore the ice and was able to breathe freely. Somewhere inside of him, he knew this was just the start of a ruthless and unsympathetic winter and many more to come. But, somehow, he was not worried. Being alive with Omar was the only thing that mattered. He sat up and stretched. In the light before dawn, the mountain peaks were colored in sugary colors of purple and baby blues. The sky was clear and so far, there was no sign of wind. He sat on the boulder and observed his surroundings.

"I am not going back, now! There is nothing to go back to, this is it!" Hakeem knelt to look closely at a five-petaled pink rosehip, it was serene and beautifully unblemished, just like their childhood, but somehow Hakeem felt repulsed by it. He threw it on the ground and then crushed it under his feet. That was strangely gratifying, he thought. Building on that same hatred, for all things pure and innocent, Hakeem and Omar eventually learned to silence the voice of their conscience and considered their becoming as the *badal.*

"You are so daring and dauntless. Brother," Omar would always tell Hakeem. He had seen his brother grow into such a strong personality, ruthless and conniving, that he was not the least bit surprised when Hakeem gained the title of chieftain in the prime age of twenty-one. Now known as *Shah*, meaning the *king*, he gave Omar, the code name *Master Qari.*

The *jihad* had begun. Hakeem knew that this version of jihad was important in the international sphere, for both the United States and the Soviets as much as the idea of a *global jihadi* was. He fought bravely against the soviets whom he considered *godless.* By the early 1990's, CIA had pumped cash stipends as high as $200,000 a month to Hakeem and his guerilla organization, along with weapons and other supplies to support their hidden agenda of Afghan communist proxy war.

"With weapons, you can tell a whole story," Hakeem told Omar. "It makes people talk. It can make the dead talk." Hakeem knew with this precise approach and strategic tactic, he could easily get both the funding and the weaponry as there were multiple US-backed agencies, bankers and governments inciting and encouraging terrorism for several reasons.

"One of the primary reasons for them to invest is the geographic location. This region bears a lot of strategic importance. And not all can control and command this land. The US government needs us here, for *their* sake!" Hakeem was right. Within months, through indirect contact, for the logistical coordination to further US positions in war-torn Afghanistan and beyond, hundreds of millions of dollars were funneled to Hakeem and his militancy. Due to this, his faction became increasingly powerful. This became the very context for Hakeem to emerge both as an indigenous southern Pashtun response to warlordism and an instrument of terror.

"Terrorism is that controlling device—whoever holds the remote owns the world!" claimed Hakeem.

Under Hakeem's patronage, the war-torn country had collapsed. Kabul and Kandahar, once the elegant cities of Afghanistan with broad streets and walled gardens tucked amid barren crags, had been pummeled by Hakeem's warlord ship into a physical ruin and human misery that compared to his charred home was equally, the worst place on earth. His Badal was to fight and blast down mud-brick blocks after blocks in his driven hatred in search of tactical advantage and Omar aka Master Qari's militia was led by the so-called Islamic scholars who systematically manipulated young children and innocent civilians into following them, blindly under the garb of religion. Hakeem used it extend his political and international influence by proselytizing to the destitute and the innocent. From that point onward, there was no more law, no more order in these areas. Scores of Hakeem's militia travelled and spread across the FATA region, along the Pak-Afghan borders, to recruit, train and teach their version of *jihad* in these districts. The villagers and local people would get harassed and brutally tortured on a daily basis by the *topaki-yaan, the men with the guns.*

The locals recalled the good times, which were now distant memories, of music parties, the get together where locals and foreigners would congregate for several days to make music, discuss poetry and literature over a cup of hot green tea and eat fish and barbeque meat. It had all turned into a distant lull, now. The abuses of Hakeem's childhood as well as the utter disregard of human life during that period, became a justification for his harsh and selfish rule as a militant commander. His core principle; *badal* and profit.

It was the same thing every day, under Hakeem's patronage---more killings and more deaths. They called him-----

"The Master and his cubs ..." the dying echoes of these powerful words channeled him back to the present moment, he moved his gaze from the moon, and turned to face the men in his tent, still carousing and drinking.

"And, you know who else was there, don't you?" Hakeem regained his self-composure and, with a laugh, swayed toward the man sitting in the shadows.

The man rose to stand beside Shah, laughing incredulously. Bahadur was stunned to see his face.

"My dear little brother." It was Omar, aka Master Qari, the devout cleric, the most religious person on the campsite, revered by all for his devotion to the holy mission of jihad.

"What is written on your chest, Qari? Should we tell all? Is it truly jihad or radicalization? You, hypocrite!" Khanan teased him.

Their boorish behavior grated on Bahadur's nerves. He could not understand why Master Qari was drunk? Why were they laughing so shamefully? He had only ever seen them dignified and restrained, as the truest soldiers, fighting in the name of righteousness. As he walked back, his mind had a million questions. *They sound so genuine and pure in their intent to fight injustice, to take badal for all the Muslim killings. Should I stay quiet, or tell everyone that they are not sincere in their cause? No! I cannot say, or they will behead me, like Mustafa. They have the power to do so! But then, that will be cowardice. What should I do?* For once, seventeen-year-old Bahadur felt the ultimate betrayal. What he just saw intruded upon and disrupted his fantasized purity of his masters' cause and mission, which promoted an impaired sense of reality in him and the rest of the children.

Perhaps, it did not matter. But in the wider scheme of things, this was the *only* thing that did matter. "Yes, it does not matter, nothing matters. I cannot run or hide. This is it! If I am staying, then what does it matter if they are sincere or not?! I have nowhere to go, no family, no friends, no one will accept or love me. I am a bomb, ready to be exploded in the hands of these masters, there is nothing waiting for me, outside of this camp. This is "home!" As he walked back, he saw two-night duty chiefs patrolling the area with their kalashnikovs. He hid behind a sandy boulder, waiting for them to pass. Bahadur had suddenly realized that there was no way out but in.

His heart was beating fast; feelings of betrayal and imprisonment led to unabated fear in his heart. This fear soon led to hatred. As a result, he became even more rebellious and defiant in his actions. He could not look at his *Amir* and masters in the same light ever again. The seed of hatred, implanted in fear grew stronger and stronger, leading to unimaginable violence and viciousness. As years passed by, Bahadur became an expert in guerrilla warfare, he'd begun as an innocent boy, and six years later was now a skilled killer, whether with guns, knives—even his bare hands. A twenty-three-year-old now, wrought into a human weapon, built expertly to dispose of the enemy. As many missions as they sent him on, he returned each time, triumphant. His name was on the FBI's *Most Wanted* list, with a five-million-dollar bounty on his head. He'd become Hakeem Shah's favorite toy, his most valued warrior, given the name "Khaakzad," which meant "son of dust" due to the destruction he inevitably left behind.

"This boy, I tell you—he turns everything to dust," Hakeem Shah would say, his voice filled with pride at the boy's transformation. Hakeem's admiration for Bahadur was not coincidental. Hakeem clearly saw his own face and childhood, in Bahadur's raptured soul.

"He is Khaakzad! The dust-bearer," they would all say, and the mountains echoed in his name.

THE SUN

August 1947.

Location: Present-day India

Kaleemullah was twelve years old when news of the Partition[9] arrived. He remembered when his friend Shamsuzzaman father, a landowner, was attacked and killed by a group of men one morning in 1947. After killing him, the men killed three women in the top floor of the house. By then, news had spread of Shamsuzzaman's father's murder. Kaleemullah's father, Feroze Khan, had campaigned in favor of Muslim League's leader Mohammad Ali Jinnah and

9 Partition: The Partition of India was the division of British India in 1947 which accompanied the creation of two independent dominions, India and Pakistan.

Pakistan in the 1946 provincial elections, and he was sure his family would become implicated in—and affected by—the Partitions' violent repercussions.

Kaleemullah was ecstatic to learn that his father was moving the family to Peshawar. He had heard so much about this "Land of the Pure" that nobody could question his intense affiliation to the word Pakistan, a name daubed on their front door. Pictures of Mohammad Ali Jinnah were pasted on the walls, and League banners along with green and white tinsel hung from the roof of their house.

The next day, while they were having lunch, their neighbor, a Sikh magistrate, came to their house, informing Feroze that a Hindu mob was coming to the area to kill Muslims. Without delay, Feroze insisted that they all begin packing to leave. Arrangements for stay over and safe travelling to Pakistan had already been made by the families of many of the Muslim military and government officers.

For more than twenty days, in constant fear of attack by the Hindu mob, they lived in a hotel compound administered and guarded by the British military. The officers took them to the railway station, and, under military guard, they traveled to Bombay. They couldn't go to Karachi directly because the security situation there was even worse. Thus, their train went via the longer route, taking more than two weeks to reach Bombay via Agra. Two other trains, which left three and four days after their own, carrying Muslim civilians to Pakistan, were attacked. Many Muslims were massacred in Patiala (in Indian Punjab) by Sikh mobs; and Kaleemullah learned that some of his friends died in the attack. Kaleemullah himself witnessed several horrifying scenes of ruthless mobs with swords attacking Muslims in the train taking them to Pakistan. For years, the memories kept him awake at night.

When they finally reached Karachi, after a three-day voyage, many of the passengers, including his father and grandfather, kissed the ground. Along with his brothers, he did the same, as the paired feelings of pride and happiness surged through his veins. Now, he knew what it meant to be a Pakistani, to have a land to claim and call his own, and to rejoice in the soil of his motherland.

After four days in a makeshift camp near Napier Road in Karachi, they took the train to Rawalpindi, then to Peshawar, where the Pakistan army was headquartered. His family was allotted accommodations, and his father Feroze resumed work with the army as a Pakistan army corps engineer. Kaleemullah joined a prominent convent school; later, he attended a British-built boarding college with his brothers, intending to serve in the army. As he grew older, he was often praised as an ideal citizen. *An ideal for young men to follow.* He spent his time studying and praying with his grandfather. With the first call of the Muezzin, he would spring out of his bed, performing his ablutions for the Dawn Prayers, even though they were not—strictly speaking—a requirement. For him, it was a gift from himself to Allah. Even after his grandfather's demise, he continued with this routine as it had now become an inseparable aspect of his entire being. And when the time came, he followed in the footsteps of his father and joined the Pakistan army. However, he was forced to resign at the young age of twenty-eight due to a spinal wound received during a UN peace mission in Bosnia. While inspecting unguarded weapons depots, his brigade was ambushed by the Bosnian Serbs who killed twenty-four of his men and injured him and four other troop members.

He returned home, bedridden for months, devastated to no longer be able to serve his country or be of any use to his aging, retired father. It seemed that the whole world had closed altogether. However, with his father's unwavering support, daylight shone through once more when Feroze endeavored to find a suitable girl for his son to marry and to bring a woman into the house. After regaining his health, Kaleemullah pursued farming on the broad swaths of land near Charsadda Road, which had been allotted to his father through the Army Welfare Trust (AWT) following his retirement.

Kaleemullah worked hard to learn farming and managed it wisely and with care, guided by the same principles followed by his father.

He helped his father to grow maize, wheat, and other grains. He dug out the waterways for irrigation with the help of two other men his father had hired. Eventually, Kaleemullah took full control of the land as his father grew old and feeble. And though there was nothing in Kaleemullah's eyes to match the glory of being an army officer, the thought of nurturing his land and shouldering the responsibilities of his father felt like a redemption of sorts.

Janat Gul was Kaleemullah's second cousin, the younger of two sisters and a brother. Her mother's home was at Nizamuddin. Her father was a brick contractor in Delhi who had decided to leave Delhi when they heard rumors that insurgents were on their way to set fire to the Nizamuddin settlement. Janat Gul, five years old at the time of Partition, migrated with her family to Karachi via Lahore from the Delhi Railway Station. They stayed in the basement of a mosque for two weeks, where she felt scared in the darkness, suffocated by the vast number of people hiding there along with them. Without light or latrines, with hardly any food or water, they huddled pitifully on the muddy ground until the Pakistan government flew in shipments of cooked rice and chapatis all the way from Lahore to feed them. Dignified Muslim professors and lawyers squeezed alongside cooks and mechanics, longtime Gandhians next to stranded, would-be Pakistani bureaucrats. The wounded and sick moaned in need of medical attention; babies were born in the open. Armed Sikhs patrolled the one choked entrance, taking down the license plate numbers of Europeans driving in to deliver food and supplies to their friends and former servants.

Finally, the train took them to Karachi, making a brief stop at Lahore. In Karachi, they stayed in the refugee camp for a few days, where Janat would fetch kerosene oil for three paisas to light the lamp and stoves in their tent. She would play *pehal dooj,* or hopscotch, with kids from the streets, and would even secretly hitch a ride on the trams of Saddar, in Karachi. There, she saw a school, but did not attend as her brother's education was prioritized. In her culture, girls' education was seen as wholly undesirable or acceptable only for a few years before puberty. The focus was mainly on marrying young and having children.

Her father finally found a local contractor job in Mansehra, and they moved there. Once she reached the age of puberty, she was home-bound, no longer allowed to go out and play. Her brother continued his schooling after their migration, and Janat and her sisters were taught to read and write at home, acquiring most of their education from their mother.

The girls were taught to remain within the four walls of their house, duty-bound, hidden away in shawls and burqas and only to go out when needed: then, only with their brother or father. Their voices were not to penetrate the walls of their house. They were the custodians of their father's honor, meant to practice living in purdah. Janat was a bright girl who liked to read.

She would secretly peer through her brother's books, whenever she'd get the chance as she knew that the pursuit of education carried penalties, some as harsh as death for the girls, so she resigned herself to her destiny, accepting her fate, always exercising discretion.

"A girl is destined for one thing only," her mother would say. "Marriage. It is a protection for us women. Someday, you will make some good man a wife, worth your weight in gold."

A spasm of fear would shoot through Janat's stomach at the thought of marrying and becoming someone's wife. What would he be like? she wondered. With her dolls, she played out marriage scenes with her sisters. They were taught sewing, and household work at an early age. The day she became engaged to Kaleemullah, Janat had been playing with her dolls in the house. There was no indication that the now sixteen-year-old was scheduled to meet her future father-in-law, until her father summoned her out of her room, setting her before a male stranger who was more than fifteen years older than Janat but, as per the cultural norms, the age difference hardly mattered.

There and then, Kaleemullah's father Feroze chose to codify the Pakhtunwali honor by marrying within his kinfolk, knowing that only a Pashtun girl would understand the true idea of rectitude. Hospitality, virtue, revenge, language, refuge—their honor extended to all these things. And though Janat Gul's father, Hikmat Yar's, poverty was well known to Feroze, he decided nonetheless to marry his son to Janat Gul, the comeliest of the sisters. Her beauty was a rare asset.

Kaleemulah knew very little about women and their emotions. His mother had died giving birth to him, and he had no sister. He was raised among men, and the only woman he knew was his grandmother, Hasan Bano. However, she had also disappeared before they could reach Pakistan during Partition riots. She had been traveling back from a family function by train, accompanied by a male servant, who upon reaching their destination could not find her in the women's compartment where he had left her. It remained unknown whether she'd left the train or was abducted. A few months later, they conducted the last rites, adding her to the list of dead ancestors. That day, Kaleemullah cried a lot as he always saw his mother in Hasan Bano, and she was the only woman left in his life. After her demise, Kaleemullah returned to his male dominated life where he remained until his marriage to Janat Gul.

A day before marriage, maidens assembled in Kaleemullah's house and sang Sandaras to the beat of drums and tambourine. Three respectable elderly women, his distant relatives, visited Janat's house a night before the marriage, dyeing her hands and feet with henna and braiding her hair into three plaits. Kaleemullah and Janat never met before marriage, nor had ever set eyes on one another. The first time Janat saw Kaleemullah, at the young age of sixteen, was from under the transparent veil of her wedding burqa, when her eyes locked on the magnetic gaze of her handsome groom, sitting behind the steering wheel, during *rukhsati.*[10] Dressed in his brown patoo shawl, there was a somber look to his swarthy face. He was very tall, had a bristling mustache and bore distant green eyes beneath close-cropped, wavy hair brushed smooth under his pakol.

Janat arrived in Kaleemullah's life amid happy songs, firecrackers, and guns fired into the air. With a thousand stars in her eyes, she sat on Kaleemullah's bed, draped now in rose and jasmine

---

10 Rukhsati: Sending off takes place when the groom and his family will leave together with the bride.

flowers. Following the Makh Katal[11] ceremony, the womenfolk presented her with gifts and money, then left the room, wishing her the best of luck.

When Kaleemullah first laid eyes on Janat, he was amazed by her innocent beauty: her skin, white as milk, her big bright eyes. He looked over her with gentle fondness, coiled up in layers of bridal clothing, her cheeks burning red as blood, her eyes downcast. He approached her gently, lifting her face with the tip of his index finger. When she finally could bear to look up at Kaleemullah, her hazel eyes appeared to him like night, of cloudless climes and starry skies; then, all that was best of dark, and light met in that gaze. It was perhaps the most beautiful night Kaleemullah had known, a communion of two pure hearts.

In the days to follow, Janat dreamt of love, turning crimson at the thought of Kaleemullah gazing over her beauty. She took care of him and his home. She served her father-in-law with all her heart when he became sick and bedridden. She had believed that Kaleemullah's love and fondness for her would only grow with each passing moment, but it was not to be. Kaleemullah did love her, but his culture and code of principles forbade him to display his affections outwardly. He was to keep his patriarchal force alive, always providing shelter and protection to his home

---

11 Makh Katal: Unveiling of face, usually done by a woman relative

and Janat. Janat, however being a sixteen-year-old, was more focused on her fantasy of being an adored wife. She tried hard at first to keep the fire of emotions alive, but the dream passed, giving way to the realities of life. A few months after their marriage, Feroze passed away, and Kaleemullah was left on his own with his father's responsibilities, becoming ever busier, with little or no time for Janat. She fulfilled her duties in service to her husband's will, honoring his stature in her life, but the time for love and folly was clearly over.

Kaleemullah was deeply religious, and Janat was forced to adhere to strict purdah and remain within the four walls of her house. And thus, her days were spent cleaning lentils or shelling peas. She would rise before sunrise and pray. She cooked and cleaned and did the laundry. And still, despite the perpetual stress of household work, despite Kaleemullah's outward lack of interest in her, it could not remove her smile. Janat knew that Kaleemullah had the utmost love and respect for her. Soon, she also accepted the fact that the blatant expression of love and emotion was not considered appropriate where he came from. She was a strong Pashtun woman, resigned to her fate from an early age. Circumstances and discomfort had never deterred her.

She showed the same fortitude when she was unable to conceive. She did not fear for her status in Kaleemullah's eyes or those of his relatives, who felt her stature fallen. She knew very well that it was traditionally imperative for her to bear a child, preferably a boy. Otherwise, Kaleemullah had all the rights to remarry as per the customs. She was a woman, and thus the failing to conceive was her fault alone, and no further consideration was required. Janat often ended her sentences with '*If Allah wills it.*' She held on to Allah, remaining steadfast for seven long years, praying, and fasting until He responded to her pleas and Zufash came into her life one cold December morning. A baby at last, the fruit of her labor, the answer to her every prayer.

And after so many years, there were no longer frown lines on Kaleemullah's forehead, and he smiled as often as she warmed his grinning face between her palms. He sang Pashtun couplets and called out to relatives. He was content, and proud, for she had given him a son. Zufash lay in the cradle as Kaleemullah leaned close to his face. The baby smiled back at him; his blue eyes so bright that it was as if he'd seized within them the whole constellation of the heavens. Placing a hand on his tiny beating heart, Kaleemullah gave Zufash the best gift of all: first, into his right ear he breathed the azan, the Muslim call to prayer; then, he moved to his other ear, declaring his son's faith.

Janat wished to name Zufash after his head-shaving ceremony, as forty days had passed. She was excited to call him by his name, but Kaleemullah was still unsure. He wanted only the best name for his son. One morning, while at work, staring toward the plummeting walls of hills and valley folds, the shining sun appeared like a jewel, illuminating the serrated peaks.

"*Zufash*!" he suddenly shouted, with all the might and air in his lungs, his voice streaming over the broad expanse of his field. Seconds later, his son's name echoed back to him, again and again, boomeranging through the blue sky above, calling down into the shadowy mountain ranges of his motherland. Every living thing heard his name. The very air of Pakistan knew his child as Zufash.

Kaleemullah squinted into the sunshine and made his way back home. Janat heard her husband's approach as he passed through the bamboo chik[12] hanging over the entrance. Kaleemullah took off his shoes, finding his son, safe and warm, staring up at him in the hammock by the kitchen, in his soft sheath of cloth. The kitchen overflowed with perfumed heat, and the scent of scattered spices and pulverized cumin seeds filled his senses.

"Your given name is Zufash, my son. Zufash. Khan. Your name rightfully means the light-bearer. The cruelty and darkness of this world is yet to touch you. Inshaa Allah, it will never succeed. You, my son, will be the envy of the darkest night. You have one life, a purposeful one, live your life well and fulfill the meaning

---

12 Chik: covering, curtain

of your name. Never be afraid, because you are my son and above all else, you are a Pathan."

And as he grew up, Zufash did feel the pride of his father flowing into him like cool spring water into an empty cistern. Kaleemullah's words dropped in Zufash's ears as if they were jewels, forever illuminating his mind and heart, showing him the way.

THE SON SHINES

The street where Kaleemulah lived was neither paved nor leveled. And so, each time it rained, six-year-olds little Zufash would wade into the muddy puddles of water, splashing around, playing games, pretending to swim. Janat chastised him then, fearing the water would make him sick, but Zufash only giggled, running over to hug her tightly. He knew as well as she it was so much bluster, her demanding exterior masking a kind and gentle heart, evident in the way she would fuss over his eating habits, in how she would mend a scrape or a bruise, in her worry when he would fall ill, and in her pride as she spoke of him to neighboring women and relatives.

"You shine like the moon, when you smile, *Ammi*," and though it happened only rarely, Zufash' silly antics were often enough for her to flash a secretive grin. Janat was tough because she was supposed to be underneath, however, there was unmistakable love and warmth, for her family meant everything to her. Zufash meant everything to her.

When he was just four and too small to venture out alone, he would spend most of his day on the roof, feet dangling over the edge, listening to the birdsongs, or the chattering of the schoolboys, or the sound of the muezzin calling the pious to pray. Their uniform and bags always fascinated his curious little mind, and he was anxious to join them, to learn about the world around him, and what lay beyond.

"Ammi, when will I go to school?" he would ask with childlike excitement. At this, Janat would only smile, and kiss his forehead. "Soon, my son, when you grow taller and stronger. Then, your Baba will take you to school."

"How soon? You mean tomorrow?"

At this, Janat would giggle and wrap him in her strong arms, the one place where Zufash felt happy, safe, and content. He would spend hours watching his mother cook, his gaze transfixed as she spread and kneaded sticky dough along a flat rock before baking it over the embers of a *cholha*[13]. He would try to help her with his tiny little hands, bringing water for her to drink and wiping the sweat from her forehead. Janat would deliberately grab him in a bear hug, wiping her sweat all over Zufash's head and cheeks as he squealed with laughter. He would help her sweep with a broom bigger than he was or bang rugs against the walls to clear the dust. But Janat always forbade him from picking up heavy objects. "Stop it, Zufash! It is too heavy, you cannot pick it up, my son," she protested, as he would roll up his sleeves and curl his fists in front of his mother to show his strength, watching in fascination the rise and fall of hard muscle, where before there had been nothing. He was sure he could feel himself growing, though he was still very small.

When Zufash turned seven, Kaleemullah began taking him to his farmland, where he would pitch in and work alongside his father, mostly collecting firewood and water in cans from the nearby stream. The fresh, cold mountain water he brought to his father first, for him to drink.

Kaleemullah had taught Zufash to be both loyal and protective, those qualities most esteemed by the Pashtun. Unlike other children his age, Zufash was growing up with a strong sense of the Pashtunwali culture. He was a serious child by nature, extremely

13 Cholha: stove

well-mannered, and known to say salaam to everyone on his street. He knew how to honor his family, including the women. He insisted on bringing in groceries and doing the outside chores, as he never liked for his mother to go out on her own. Even at the tender age of seven, he insisted on escorting her.

It was a source of pride for him. He considered himself the man of the house in his father's absence, the one to always protect his family's honor.

"You are the queen of this house, Ammi Jaan. Your place is here, not outside," he would say in a polite and caring voice. At this Janat would only look at him, overflowing with love.

"If I stay indoors all the time, then who will bring things from the outside? Who will take care of the household, and bring you back from school? Your Baba is at his farm, and sometimes doesn't come back for days."

"I will! I will do it for you, *Ammi*! Baba asked me to take care of you when he is away. I am a big boy now." He would stick his tiny chest out and stand tall, shoulders back.

At this, Janat couldn't help but laugh.

When he turned eight, he had already learnt five siparahs[14] of the Holy Quran by heart; he also offered prayers five times a day. Kaleemullah registered him in the Army school, in hopes that

---

14 Siparahs: one of thirty parts of varying lengths into which the Quran is divided.

his son would join the Pak army and fulfill his father's dreams. Zufash loved going to school, unlike some of his other friends, who considered it little more than a monotonous set of routines, from seven in the morning until noon. Often, he would wake up as early as five-thirty in the morning, which was easier during the summer months, but became intolerable in the winter season. In the dark and rainy dawn, it was harder for him to leave his warm blanket to perform his ablutions.

Janat made a point of lighting the water heater early in the morning, so her son would not have to wash himself with cold water. She would rouse Zufash out from his bed in the silence of the dawn when the only sound he could hear was the hissing of the water-heater or the boiling tea kettle.

He would then join his father for prayers and to recite the Quran, sitting beside him, while Janat prepared his breakfast and lunch box. She helped him dress, checking his nails and brushing his curly hair while reciting '*surahs*[15]' on him and instructing him to be safe and obey the teacher and eat his lunch. He would unquestionably follow these rules, nod dutifully, bobbing his head endlessly to assuage his mother.

School was a time for studying, but also fun, and he had a lot of friends. His two best friends were Safi and Haidar. Safi

---

15 Surah: a chapter in the Quran

was the son of a head constable. He was taller than Zufash, with a kind demeanor.

"Come over here Zufash. I will buy you coke and samosa for lunch." Safi would always insist on sitting beside Zufash, bothering him throughout the lessons by cracking jokes, or elbowing him to make him laugh. "Stop it, Safi, you will get me in trouble with Miss!" Zufash would whisper back. Haidar, by contrast, was quiet and introverted.

Perhaps that was because he came from a poorer family, his father a lower division clerk in the army regimental center. Further, he had four other sisters, and his responsibilities had caused him to mature early. Already, he knew he needed to become successful to support his father and marry off his four sisters. Thus, left to his own, he would be studying all the time. "Come now, Haider, give yourself a break! Study, study that is all you do." Zufash and Safi made sure this wasn't the case, shoving him out of his work and toward the canteen, helping him to forget his worries, at least for a while.

They would meet up regularly to play football, seven stones, hide-and-seek, and all manner of games. At the close of the school day, in their last break, they would sit together on the ground, eating hot samosas and drinking cold Coke, joking around, enjoying conversations and laughter.

Zufash would always find his father waiting for him at the school gate as soon as he finished. "Baba!" He would call out to him breathlessly, racing to jump into his arms. On the way home, he told stories of his day, about his teacher giving him a star, what he did with his friends as he rested his chin on his father's head. Sometimes, he would even sleep while on Kaleemullah's shoulders, if too tired. Kaleemullah would walk real slow, once he would realize that Zufash has slept. Otherwise, he listened attentively, caught up in Zufash's youthful excitement.

"One day, when I am old, my son, you will carry all my burdens, just like I am carrying you, right now. You will take care of your mother and the nest that I have built, you are my pride." Kaleemullah's hopes and dreams were all dependent on Zufash.

And Zufash could not wait to share all his adventures with his father. They shared a common ground of family concern and pride.

Once they were home again, Zufash would eat his lunch and then sleep for a while. He always felt drowsy after a long school day. Janat would wake him for his afternoon prayers; following this, he spent time on the veranda with her before going out to play with his friends, who also lived in the same neighborhood. After nine o'clock, he would eat his dinner, then sit at the small table in his room and study in the light of his small lamp until Janat brought a glass of warm milk with honey, urging him to sleep.

"Time for bed," Janat would say softly, closing his books.

"But *Ammi*, I have a science test tomorrow, I must score the highest—at least beat Safi and Haidar," Zufash resisted, though mildly. He was a smart boy, such that he only needed to scan his books once to know what was in them, after which he would earn a position in his class.

"Your head will ache if you study this much—come now! I will massage almond oil into your scalp, and you'd better not say anything."

At this Zufash would smile and obey her respectfully. Seated on a stool in the kitchen, Janat would massage the hot oil into his hair. Her fingers danced along his scalp, pulling apart his soft curls, every brush of the comb an indulgence. She knew every inch of his head, as she massaged the stress and worries away. She would press her lips to his every scab, every contusion, everywhere. He would then go and sit with his father after Isha prayers, listening to stories, relishing in his counsel. That was his favorite time of the day.

"You make me and your Zoor *aba*[16] proud, my son. If he was ever alive to see you, you'd be his favorite. I hope you grow up to be strong and brave. I want you to serve your country one day, so your Baba and Zoor aba may salute you from the heavens above."

---

16 Aba: grandfather

Kaleemullah's hazel flecked eyes shone brightly each time he'd look at Zufash, offering his son a curt salute, which Zufash returned.

And why shouldn't he feel proud? Zufash was his only son. His blood, his life.

Zufash's childhood, as a pathan child, was one of make-believe ferocity, and he was never without a plastic gun or sword. Playing *chor police*[17] with his friends, he always chose to be the police officer, escaping into a safer, more containable world of fierceness than many of the others. However, in the real world, he was still only a seven-year-old boy.

His naïve and innocent life kept his tiny heart filled with joy; however, he was intelligent enough to be aware not just of his own existence, but also of his surroundings. He grew anxious when, to his surprise, Janat forbade him from going out at night, or when Kaleemullah spoke angrily about the religious insurgents and their terror tactics intended to harm his motherland, how they were taking Peshawar in the wrong direction, denigrating the name of Islam and the Pashtunwali code they lived by.

"This is too much now," Kaleemullah complained to his friend, Gulwali, one evening. They were sitting on a *charpoy*[18] underneath

---

17 Chor Police: kids' game on robbery and chase

18 Charpoy: wooden cot

the Mango tree in Kaleemullah's verandah, smoking *hookah*[19] in the cloudy weather. It had been raining since morning. The rain covered everything in a gauzy white haze, like a winter fog. The rain had finally stopped but the low hanging clouds still blotted out the star lit sky. The two friends continued to enjoy the cold of the night while chatting about pressing matters.

"May Allah's wrath fall on these infidels, for what religion do they follow? How do they even dare recite the *kulma*—they are anything but *musalman*, wallahi[20]! The killing of one human being is considered akin to the killing of all mankind. In the Quran, we are instructed not to harm the plants and the animals, even in times of war. And these so-called custodians of our *rasool's* faith (peace be upon HIM) faith . . . they humiliate women, kill children, abuse the elderly—tormenting, relishing in the agony of others—in the name of *Jihad*? I fail to understand, Gulwali, what the Quran do they read?

Do they even know the true meaning of Jihad? Has the Pashtun blood become so thinned that they should now raise their fists against women and children?"

Kaleemullah's voice burst in anger, enraged at the turn of events in his country. His friend Gulwali, whom he had met

---

19 Hookah: an oriental tobacco pipe with a long, flexible tube which draws the smoke

20 Wallahi: by God

during his army days in Bosnia, tried to appease him. Gulwali was a retired ISPR officer and had much insight and understanding of the current affairs in the country. Kaleemullah and Gulwali's friendship had only grown stronger through the years.

"I know Lalay[21], I know, but what to do? Things drastically changed around here after the Cold war. The Talibs zooming across the city in Pajeros in Toyotas laden with heavily armed men flaunting weapons. No police or army to stop them as Taliban forces grew stronger. Do you remember? "He inquired, his eyes looking, in the distant past.

"Yes, I remember all too well…. How, overnight, Mercedes buses from Afghanistan replaced wagons and other vehicles. My uncle's restaurant was pushed out of business by the new Afghan eateries. My father told me not to wear pants and a shirt. It was replaced by beards and skullcaps. And the city became frozen in fear and uncertainty. And, here we are now, worse than before." Kaleemullsah, shook his head in despair.

"They are at the extreme end of ignorance, Kaleem. Now, we are living in such times that when one group decides to kill some random people on the roads or in the park one day, in the name of God, others follow suit. You remember Shamir? My ex-colleague? His son Moktar was killed in last year's Taliban attack, the blast in

---

21 Lalay: dear friend

the community park, here in Peshawar. Poor guy! Was out there with his kids and wife. They all died. Shabbir was inconsolable. He ultimately left the country." Gulwali passed his hand through his white beard gently while staring at the gracefully swirling wet branches of the Mango tree.

"Oh, my Allah! What pain, what a loss, for a father. You are right, Gulwali. Just as "Pakistan" translates to *Land of the Pure,* "Afghanistan" means *Eternal Waiting*— There were times when people from both sides had one common bond of interest. Our grand bazaars were the easiest place to lose oneself, to forget and to disappear into the labyrinth of narrow alleys. Among the gateways, stalls, and miniature taverns, I remember my grandfather and his companions, hiding from the burning sun, fortifying themselves as they leisurely drank their qahwa, chewing pressed tobacco with an added dash of opium, and smoking bubbling hookahs. But now, we crave for a moment of peace. Our lives, our children's lives are all at stake." Kaleemullah looked up at the sky, reminiscing the lost memories of a time he truly craved to hold onto, once more.

"It has all changed now, lalay! Peshawar is now like a man torn apart by a quandary: full of fears, incapable of making a choice. Who thought that a city with a legendary spirit would be torn apart by the Taliban?" Gulwali put his hands up toward the sky, in hopelessness. "But, let me tell you some inside intel, straight from the army." Gulwali leaned forward and whispered. "This goes beyond the confines of Northwest Pakistan. Most of these so-called jihadists are not even true Muslims, unlike the mujahidin, who raise arms only to protect and uphold the sanctity of our lives and faith. The recent army operation, you know of the Pakistan army, caught some of the insurgents and asked them to recite a few verses from the Quran. You would not believe what my friends at the Headquarters told me…" Their conversation was interrupted by Janat's voice who beckoned Kaleemullah from the kitchen that the Qahwa was ready. Gulwali held the Qahwa with the right cuff of his pheran and took a sip with a slurping sound. The scent of the Qahwa spread throughout the entire veranda, burying the damp odor of the Mango tree.

"Uncle Gul!" Their talks were interrupted by Zufash's excited shout, for his favorite uncle was there. He ran towards Gulwali with all the speed and haste of youth. His clothes were still drenched wet from playing all day long in the rain and his bright dark hair glistened with the rain drops.

"Here is my hero! Come here, my sher[22], how have you been? Guess what I brought you this time?" Gulwali rubbed his fingers affectionately against Zufash's head.

The boy's eyes gleamed with excitement. "A toy car? A rocket?

---

22 Sher: lion

Bat and ball? Scrapbook? What, what, Uncle Gulwali?" Zufash cried, hopping lightly with excitement. A gleam of pure love and joy passed over Gulwali's face as tenderly and excitedly Zufash asked for the toy, and expressed such hopes as affection hopes.

"It is an officer uniform or your school's dress down day, next week! Go now quickly, put it on, and show me how Officer Zufash would salute his Uncle Gulwali." He looked up at Zufash's innocent face with a strong expression of love and adoration.

Zufash nodded, running back inside as the men continued their conversation.

"The terrorist, caught by the army last week during Operation Zarb-e-Azb[23], did you see his interview on the television?" Gulwali asked, squeezing another lemon into his qahwa, and mixing the contents together.

"The one who was caught for planning the attack on Jinnah International Airport in Karachi?" Kaleemullah asked, taking a sip from his cardamom tea.

"Yes! That one. He could not even recite *kulma* properly, he could only say *Allah Akbar*—even then, only in his weird Chechen accent. He knew nothing about the cardinals of the Koran or any surah. All he said was that he was jihadi. When asked about the

---

23 Zarb-e-Azb: Operation Zarb-e-Azb was a joint military offensive conducted by the Pakistan Armed Forces against various militant groups.

three forms of jihad and if he knew that the most sublime of it all was *Jihad al nafs*—struggle against the self— he scrunched his nose and squinted his eyes, very much like my three-year-old son Waleed does when he hears a new word." Gulwali shook his head, disappointment in his voice.

"It is the end of times, Gulwali, they are tarnishing the true Pashtun name." Kaleemullah sniffed. "The whole thing makes my blood boil, really. The state is no longer functional. They are undermining the social, political, and national infrastructure. Yes! You are right. Most of these attacks are perpetrated by the youth, Gulwali! They are destroying our future, targeting the most vulnerable. I wish dearly that my injury hadn't forced me to retire from the Pak army, for I would have fought alongside my men in Zarb-e-Azb until my last breath . . . to save innocent people from their atrocities." Kaleemullah clenched his fists, pressing his knuckles into his forehead until both were white.

Zufash returned, clad in a khaki uniform, with medals and stars on his chest and shoulders. He wore a green peaked cap with a star and crescent on it, both the adornments and the child's face glowing like the moon itself. He saluted his father and uncle before landing in his uncle's embrace. Gulwali kissed his forehead.

"Ah! My soldier! See, Lalay, our beloved son Zufash will fulfill this wish of yours, Insha Allah. Just look at him!" Gulwali held Zufash out in front of him, taking him by both shoulders, looking over the little soldier carefully. "He is growing up so beautifully, so good-looking, dutiful, and resilient. He will be your pillar, your strength. Mark my words, Kaleemay—this boy of yours will make you proud. He will keep your turban as high as your head is!"

Gulwali was right about Zufash. But Kaleemullah's brow was furrowed, his face was strained with fear for his son and the safety of his home. The entire community was living in increased dread of the escalated tensions between the Pak army and the Taliban militants. Every now and then a blast could be heard, or the *duz-duz* sound of an AK-47 on the streets beyond.

Zufash's friends at school also told him of their parents' fears of the terrorists, these *bad people,* against education and progress. Men who abused women, sentencing them to death for pursuing any ambition beyond the roles of dutiful wife and daughter, for nothing more than daring to dream. It made Zufash curious about these so-called terrorists, but with no real understanding as to why someone would want to hurt or kill another human being; in his mind, they simply became a vague, nebulous fear.

At the end of the day, Zufash slept soundly beneath a star-filled sky, tucked safely in his bed. Janat checked on him often at night, and fixed his blanket when he kicked it off, pulling the covers over his shoulders to keep him from shivering before closing her arms around him, to hug him once more. This was Zufash's world, a tranquil place where every day was gentle and soulful, and where each held a reverence and love for the other. These were mild winter evenings whose spring-like bloom had inspired many to leave their barred windows ajar or sleep outside, in the veranda.

The little neighborhood was always filled with the sounds of children playing, of distant hawkers selling eggs and tea and car horns and the smell of exhaust fumes and the neighbor's cooking, all wafted in. Zufash would know instantly what aunty Samina next door had cooked through the aroma. He would spring into action and rush to their neighbor's home to eat his favorite biryani or *aloo keema*.

"I knew you were coming." Aunty Samina would always greet him with a hug and a smile. Most days were like this, ordinary but carrying love and affection, smiles hanging like congruous portraits between neighbors. They all looked after each other, like a knitted community. Everyone was considered either an **aunt** or an **uncle**. All children were treated by the elders as their own. There was khala Samina in the left house and chacha Pervez in the right. Then a few houses away, there was aunty Amina, puller of cheeks, maker of treats, who would conveniently thrust herself in, to see Janat over a cup of hot tea.

The only other place, where he felt as safe and as loved, was his school. After crossing the utter chaos and noisy streets of the city, into the school gate, he felt protected and shielded, like in his mother's arms. The lush green trees on either side of the road leading up to his class in the elementary wing welcomed him. His friends would call out to him and the excitement on his face, thinking about all the fun and play, was truly unmatched. His teachers adored him, and his little heart would dance in joy, every day in the second safest place, on earth.

DUST CLAD KHAAK

Present Day

Location: Militant Camp, Nawaz Kot, South Waziristan

"Louder, boy. Louder!" cried another of the black turbans, as the rest heckled and mocked.

"I am a sinner. I did not offer my Zuhr prayers. I am sick, and felt nauseous, so I lay down for a bit, behind the big rock," the young man mumbled submissively.

The turban roared with laughter, rubbing his hand on his hennaed beard, turning to the rest of the men, his voice ringing out as clearly as the tolling of a bell. "Astaghfirullah! You deserve thirty lashes for disobeying your masters and prioritizing yourself over Allah. Let this be an example to all, whoever wishes to denounce our laws and disobey Allah, this will be their fate. Allah ho Akbar!" He lifted a heavy reed high into the air and brought it down across the young boy's back with a loud slap, slicing into the skin as the boy writhed in pain. Shrugging away his scary mane of orange hair, he hit the boy again, then again, as the other men in the crowd counted.

The young boy fell in a heap, his back an oozing mess of blood, dripping and daubing the fabric of his flak jacket. His breath came in short, rasping pants, interspersed with cries of pain that pierced the subterranean vaults of the high Hindu Kush Mountains. The fifteen minutes of abuse seemed never ending.

"Khaakza . . . oh, Khaakza! Come over here, see how this one's squealing like a girl! Aye, khabeesa."[24] The boy saw the black turban's eyes were filled with a wild, primeval glow as he called out to a rugged-looking young man seated on a boulder, away from the crowd, his head down as he cleaned the barrel of his Russian-made AK- 47 across his lap. Though the temperature was nearly sixty degrees Celsius, he seemed unaffected by the heat.

Nearly twenty-three years of age, he wore a standard black shemagh[25] that fanned out above his head, and black kohl rimmed his green eyes as they flicked up ominously, like a hawk watching

---

24 Khabees: rascal

25 Shemagh: headdress fashioned from a square scarf, usually made of cotton.

his prey with an unflinching gaze, his jaw firmly set, ever ready and always alert. Frown lines appeared on his forehead; vertical slashes entwined between thick eyebrows. There was a visible cut above his left eyebrow—shrapnel from a rocket-propelled grenade that had driven all the way to the bone, leaving another jagged scar across his aquiline nose. There was no smile on his lips, set so tightly as to be barely visible, as his hands moved mechanically over the weapon, dirty and bruised fingers moving swiftly and surely.

The boy felt fear running down his spine, just by looking at Khaakza.

But Khaakza was not concerned with the *cleansing* of the recruit for skipping his prayers. He had seen it before, many times— he'd gone through it himself. It was almost mandatory, a ritual that would carry on and on like the spinning of a wheel. He saw the other young recruits, mostly aged six to ten, watching in horror; clearly, they took no pleasure in it either, though knew better than to say anything about it. Nor were they allowed to shield their eyes. Now, their expressions were blank, their eyes confused, but their lips not daring to question the masters. Khaakza knew that look; once, he'd worn it himself. He continued with his business in a calm silence.

The black turban lunged toward him, a short man made taller by the traditional headdress he wore, his face red with rage as he drew his Kalashnikov up to Khaakza. "Aye, *khabeesa* . . . when Ghulam calls out to you, you obey, there and then! You may be Commander Hakeem's favorite, but to me you are nothing more than the filth of the earth. I will suffer no attitude from you and could finish this right now by putting a bullet into your head!" Ghulam turned around to ask the crowd of boys, his tone derisive, his face gloating. "What do you say, huh? What do you think, boys? Shall we kill Prince Khaakza right now? It would be fun to watch."

Ghulam might have continued with his sneering threats, but Khaakza had had enough. Placing his AK-47 aside, he stood up, facing the man. Over six feet tall and dressed in mud patched shalwar kameez and a flak jacket, the thump of his heavy black mountaineering boots echoed loudly in the chamber as Khaakza stepped forward. He did not say a word, only extended his arm, pressing the muzzle of Ghulam's gun against his chest—daring him to shoot.

Ghulam's skin began to burn on his neck as he tried to pull his gun away, but Khaakza did not let him. Filled with rage, Ghulam spat on Khaakza's face. "You know, what is the best thing about you, *khabeesa*? You come from a whore mother," he sneered. "Yes! You heard me right, you think you are some sort of a prince, well guess what? You are a bastard son of a bastard king!" Ghulam began to laugh through stained and rotted teeth, a haggard sound, like gravel under boots.

His laughter hit Khaakza's nerves like fingernails scraping a chalkboard, and the palm of his hand burned against the cool metal of his dagger. His heart pounded, squeezing more and more blood with each beat, flooding his eyes, and making his skull throb. Before Ghulam could utter another word, the butt of Khaakza's blade slammed into his cheek; a moment later, it slashed over Ghulam's face, across his right eye, slicing deeply all the way down to his jaw.

Ghulam stood still for a moment, in shock, his remaining eye wide, his gun held out loosely before him. Then, a fountain of blood sprayed across Khaakza's face, as Ghulam's jaw snapped and hung loose, broken. He fell to the dusty ground, howling and screaming, his spine arching, thrusting into the air in his agony. Blood poured out of his ravaged eye socket, gushing over his cupped hands as he pressed them to his face.

Khaakza approached slowly, hunching down beside the man now moaning like a dog, spitting out a mess of broken lip, blood, and teeth. Ghulam collapsed then, wriggling in a pool of blood while deep, guttural profanities streamed like the blood from his ravaged mouth.

"I've grown tired of your preaching style anyway," Khaakza

said in a whisper, "for it has become so . . . bland. This will put you back on track." Then he turned and walked away slowly. Three other turbans ran to Ghulam's aid as Khaakza approached the young boys, huddled together, witnessing all with incredulous faces.

"Come on, boys, it is time for your lesson with Master Qari." He passed a cold, fleeting look at the thirteen-year-old, whose back was now slashed with marks and caked with drying blood. He approached the boy, pulling him up by his hair. The boy radiated heat, hot as a boiling kettle. His mouth was parched, his lips leathery. His heart thudded crazily against his flak jacket, and his breath came in short, rasping pants. His senses were disoriented due to the torture he endured while the thumping of blood pulsated in his ears. He tried getting up and fell again, the pain having seemed to take away his very sight. His muscles ached and burned; his feet felt so heavy that it seemed impossible for him to walk.

Khaakza saw himself in that boy, roiling in pain; the only difference was, no one had come to his aid as he once lay upon the ground, helpless and bleeding.

"Get up, boy, drink some water," Khaakza demanded, holding up his canteen and thrusting the wet, cool mouth of the sack against the boy's parched lips. He guzzled from the bottle like he had never tasted water before. "What's your name?"

"Naqi . . . Naqibullah!" The boy could hardly speak.

Khaakza's stern face softened a little; something in the aspect of the pitiful creature before him must have touched his heart. Then he spoke to the boy, as though to himself. "Today is your first day, Naqibullah. Mark your wounds carefully because there will be many more to come! You may be promised heaven in the afterlife, but make no mistake, you *will* go through hell first. *Desert of Death!* It means hell on earth. That is the name given to this place. Have you ever been to hell, Naqibullah?"

The boy shook his head.

Khaakza moved his eyes slowly over the treacherous landscape, scrutinizing every inch of the area surrounding them. It was getting darker now with the increasing wind blowing the gritty dust into their eyes, a tendency of thinking about survival awoke in Khaakza's mind as he spoke.

"You will bleed every day, Naqibullah! You will have so many questions, so much confusion, so much more pain—and hatred. You will only be told that you are bleeding for Allah and for his defenders as you are punished. And your body will compensate. Your skin will grow cold and blue with wounds, your eyes will dilate, and the tiny vessels of your brain will slowly begin to suffocate. Your lungs will be desperate for air. Your veins will be constricted. Death will seem imminent as you'll hang on, fighting through the haze, to survive, to breathe—endure. Then, just when you believe that all is lost, a new life will be presented to you, filling you up with cleansed blood and bringing forth the testimony of the heavens, as we all are promised. Do you understand now, boy? You do not need to go to hell when you are already living in one!"

Khaakza pressed his forehead against the boy's, his eyes fixed on Naqi's innocent face. Naqibullah looked up, tears clouding his vision. Tears of utter despair, contracting his heart, congealing the blood in his eyes. Khaakza's unflinching gaze met with Naqibullah's tear-filled eyes and dragged him into his own, small corner of hell.

Khaakza had once had emotions, too; he remembered them well. He had cried at nearly everything when he was first brought to the camps. Soon enough, however, he came to realize that crying, smiling—feeling any emotions—was only a hindrance.

He took Naqibullah to the washing area, where he was given a proper bath and the ubiquitous white cotton shalwar kameez to wear along with a white prayer cap. This was the garment Naqibullah would wear until he reached the promised golden gates of heaven with silken robes throughout eternity. Khaakza was familiar with this narrative structure; he believed in it once, too, including a happy ending. But not anymore. He had stopped believing, a long time ago.

***

It was around nine o'clock in the evening when Ghulam entered the commander in chief Hakeem Shah's chamber, all battered and bruised, to show him what had occurred earlier in the day. Hakeem Shah was busy lining up a new cadre of die-hard commanders to take on Pakistani security forces considering the ongoing military operations with Master Qari and Khanaan when Ghulam interrupted him with his outburst regarding Khaakza.

"He did this! Your beloved Khaakza!" Ghulam cried. "With the same knife you gifted him, after he assassinated Mehsud! Hakeem Shah, you must put a leash on him. I am your second in command, after all. He is getting out of control. Look what he did to me! Who will respect me now?" Ghulam pointed to his blind eye, now covered by the black patch, his wounds crudely stitched, as he cringed, seething with rage.

"I will tell him to obey you when you stop being a bagairat[26]! Now, stop moaning like a girl and man up! Own your beating, you couldn't put up a proper fight if you tried. He is Khaakzad—whatever he touches turns to dust. The men told me how conveniently he slashed you open, like a gutted sheep! Therefore, I like him, for he is fearless and brave. He destroys his enemy without a second thought, and you could learn a thing or two from him."

---

26 Bagairat: Scumbag

Shah raved about Khaakza as Ghulam's face turned to cinders. Khanaan and Qari could be seen laughing in the background.

They all knew of Hakeem's attachment to Khaakza, ever since he had been brought to the camp. Hakeem grew fond of Khaakzad as the years passed, having seen the little boy grow and transform into a weapon. There was something about Khaakza that he seemed to adore—a rawness in his demeanor. His eyes were bright and intelligent and his reactions . . . always different from the rest. He was difficult to handle as he grew into a teenager. Shah had seen him punished, seen his indifference while being stripped naked, a knife at his neck, a silent threat to conform. It did not stop Khaakza from fighting, thrashing until they whipped him nearly senseless. There was something that drove the boy to such a vicious rebellion. Shah could not tell what it was as Khaakza would not utter a word. Shah had seen his silent fists and fingernails, gouging mercilessly. Even when his limbs would refuse to obey him, and the taste of dust and straw and metallic tang of blood would fill up his mouth—still he attempted to put up a fight. It was as if pain had settled like a stone in his gut, blending with a stark indifference.

Hakeem Shah admired the boy's courage. Shah kept an eye on his every move as time passed. It seemed as if he was saving Khaakza for something bigger—something special.

"Forget about him Shah, he is always moaning like a girl! We all know, he is jealous of Khaakza," Khanaan said spitefully.

"Oh, not jealous, Khanaanay! Everybody here is afraid of the boy's courage. I admire its rawness. I see myself in him. Bitter, full of hate and ready to detonate, anytime. Sheer aggression." Shah made a fist to show his admiration for Khaakza's fearlessness.

"I know you admire the boy, Shah. But right now, we have more pressing matters to discuss. That is why I gathered everyone here for you." Khanaan continued, worried in his eyes.

"The Pakistan army has done enough damage in their territory areas, destroying many of our campsites and villages in the past months. They have killed hundreds of our men in Mirali! Strikes are currently taking place in the Boya tehsil, Degan forests, and Datta Khel tehsil of North Waziristan. According to the intel, they are planning to send some thirty thousand troops in the next six months for a major ground offensive."

"And also…" Qari added, intently. "I just heard news that the Afghan Taliban have rejected our dawa and have refused to take part in this mission. We do not need them, anyway. We cannot wait any longer to persuade them. Our commandos, who conducted the all-night siege of Karachi airport, and was also killed in the Mirali operation. We need to stop the Pakistan army from launching the ground offense, Shah! You might want to inform the higher-ups of this matter, so they can pressure Pakistan from the top. Upsurge the drone attacks, to create a decoy! Strike a blast or two. They will surely cede to pressure or be distracted by their petty rows with the U.S., in defense of their sovereignty. That will surely buy us time!"

"Six, fifty-six, hundred and twenty, hundred and sixty—" Undisturbed by their strategic blubbering, Shah counted as he inspected the deserted landscape from his compound's window. His companions stared at him in confusion. "More than twelve hundred innocent civilians killed by suicide bombers, just this year, and look at them! Still standing strong, still breathing, and surviving! If I have learned anything from my dialogues and observations, it is that the Pakistani people are tough to the bone—it is not easy to break their nerves, their morale. *Heart!* That is where the softness is! They are highly emotional—aim for their heart, it will break them. But remember, if you miss, they *will* come after you, no matter if you hide in the deepest abyss of hell, they will hunt you down and kill you! When the country is engulfed by political dishevel and revolutionary jalsas, this is the right time to strike for us as per my sources inside the country." Hakeem Shah's deep voice resonated in the room.

Heart? Hmm, what could it be? They all wondered together.

They weighed all possible options. They were not looking for an easy victory; they did not expect any of the recruits to come back alive. That was their last concern. They just wanted to hit where it would hurt the most, to cause uncertainty, unrest, and fear in the public and the army. Something that would tear their hearts and shred their morale into tiny fragments.

"Children! Let us kill . . . their *children*!" Master Qari clapped and jumped a little at the sudden epiphany.

Ghulam finally chimed in, a dark and vicious look in his eyes. "*Zabardast*[27] Qari, but we cannot just kill their children only, can we? What if . . . we attack their schools? This way, we can kill those rats in hordes. The more dead bodies, the better!"

"Sounds like a perfect plan! The more their kids should bleed, should writhe in pain, the better! People will blame the U.S. war on terror, and the government will bulldoze the army and ISI to shield their own incompetence. The army will blame the enemy "within", the blame-game will begin. Then the *S-wing*[28] will come to us for treaties and negotiations. And, this time, we will concede, to stop the ground offense," said Qari, his mouth carved into a conceited smile.

Khanaan was agitated by Qari's pompous display of such

---

27 Zabardast: Excellent

28 S-wing: A secret organization within ISI, largely composed of supposedly retired military and ISI officers, which does not officially exist, and which handles relations with radical elements.

limited information. His arrogance for being Shah's brother might have had an influence in the brainwashing field, but when it came to premeditated Intel and tactical insight, Khanaan was Shah's right hand.

"Why do you think, Qari, that the Pakistan army has regained control over Swat Valley? Attacking our safe havens and targeting our training camps while the U.S. is still out there, crying in front of the world about the lack of support on Pakistan's part while she conducts an occasional drone strike, one that has a far greater chance of killing a *Baraat*[29] than us? I suggest you do your homework first before you make such foolish assumptions. Otherwise, focus on what you do best misleading the little minds." Khanaan's voice dripped with sarcasm. Master Qari's usual calm demeanor had faded as he was stung by the insult. Before he could retaliate,

Ghulam reached out and latched onto Qari's arm.

"Khanaan is right, Qari," Ghulam said forcefully as he glanced over Khanaan. "But he is judging you on the wrong playing field. Let me ask you a question worthy of your standards. If you cannot find a single verse or hadith about killing children as a part of Jihad in Islam, how will you authenticate this as a religious feat, to them and to the world?"

---

29 Baraat: Wedding procession

"You fool!" Qari roared, his voice ricocheting off every surface in the chamber, forcing everyone to fall very still under his outraged threat. "If Islam is the measuring stick, then you will not find a *single* verse on killing anyone without reason! As for the hadith, they are not the source of jurisprudence in Islam. Many reasons have been fabricated, to suit purposes such as ours. The bulk of the Quran is about worshiping Allah and living a kind, peaceful life, but would that sell? Is it worth hijacking? Of course not!" Qari's cutting and spiteful words jangled in their ears as he continued.

"But, what about the verses on war and Jihad?" Ghulam asked Qari, teasingly.

"Oh, yes! The verses on war! It should be clear to you that a true sacred text on the permissibility of jihad is insufficient to trigger mass brutality unless other conditions are present as well. Think twice before you ask me to find one to your liking! In that case, the Bible and Torah contain such violent verses on war too! The crusades were fought ostensibly in the name of the Christian Holy Spirit, and those were some of the most violent wars in the history of this world."

"We are not fighting the crusades, Qari," Khanaan retorted, in a much more reconciled tone of voice. "What does it matter which religion one follows—Muslim, Jew, or Christian—so long as it can be used to delude people and divide them? Lack of religious understanding regarding such matters helps us."

"But we *are* fighting the crusades, you fool!" Qari shot back irritably. "Our job is to make people live in fear, to hide so our makers can run and operate the world order. The funniest part is that you ask me to justify the killing of these children! Do you know why this is funny?" Qari had regained his composure and was leaning against the wall, resting his head on his forearm. "Because most of these vicious acts are sponsored by the very same people who conveniently propagate this religion as *violent*. This fact is so transparent; it needs no justification. You only need to say: You kill our children, we kill yours! The moment we first proclaimed ourselves to kill in the name of Islam, when we became identifiable to its name—we became the antithesis! This world is blind, and we have conveniently lent our eyes for them to see. They will believe whatever we show them. And, when it comes to money, power and greed, it is such a poisonous coercion that people within will sell us the very intel and share their two cents on how to intercept and kill these children; their very own people. Needless to say, next time, think twice before calling me foolish!" His tone was venomous as he stood tall before Khanaan, his eyes dark as pitch. "You may know about war and its hidden conspiracies. You may have Intel, boy, but I know the father of it all—religion!" Qari had shifted from his dull shock to his usual arrogant exclamation. Khanaan shrugged his shoulders and looked past him to Shah.

"What are your orders, *Amir*? Will the think-tanks object to this?" Hakeem Shah's massive forehead was wrinkled, as if the sound of their argument caused him pain. When he spoke, however, it was evident that he had followed the conversation well enough.

"From dust to ashes!" Hakeem said, in his usual authoritative tone. "First, they create us by destroying everything that we own, our homes, our families in the name of war, then they train us, and feed us, and then expect us to bark and bite at their enemies. To bark, to bite, to sacrifice—and then to be hunted!" said Hakeem, laying one hand on the table and bending toward Qari and Khakaan, face nearly as pallid as their own with anger. He then continued, assertively.

"Focus on the offense, I will take care of the rest , I have people working on the inside, they will show us the way in." They all nodded silently that they understood; none of them questioned this man; not today, not ever.

THE BLACK MOON

The morning of November 07 broke bright and shining. As was his custom after waking up, Hakeem walked out onto his training compound's terrace to take in the spectacular view of the plots hatched on the dusty plains of Nawaz Kot. He was enjoying his opium-scented *qahwa* when Ghulam entered with an important piece of information. He was very happy with the planning, ordering of his commanders to gain intel on the APS School in Peshawar. He had his militants there to spy, willingly assisting in facilitating the plan, creating decoys, providing maps, access points, and timings. All was decided, right down to the lodging to safely harbor Shah's chosen men.

"We are ready with our blueprint, Hakeem!" Ghulam continued. "We have intel that the government officials had been warned and made aware by their intelligence services that an attack on Army Public School may happen. There is a likelihood they may have beefed up the security or bolstered the precincts and the walls around the gates, but per our inside source, they have disregarded that document and the warning. All is good to go."

"What about the seven recruits, Ghulam? Where is that list that I have asked you to compose?" Shah reminded him, while looking at the dusty vistas of the dilapidated town.

"Oh, I have it here! Seven of our best men." Ghulam boasted a list of names. "Sadulayev will be the leader of the group. He is sharp and aggressive, having served in the Caucasus Front and killed a hundred and thirty-eight men in the 2005 Nalchik raid. Sadulayev will be accompanied by Zawal and Abdul—both are Zillikhel Wazir—tough to the bone. Zahid and Ressam, from the Khalden training camp, are well trained in light and heavy weaponry, sabotage, target selection, and guerilla warfare tactics. They can take down an army of men—the children won't stand a chance," Ghulam said, savagely.

"What about the other two men?" Shah took the list from Ghulam and gave it a passing look.

"One of them is a minor; his name is Naqibullah. He joined us just a few months back. We will use him as a decoy, and he will blow himself up, Master Qari has him ready!" Ghulam gave a derisive smile to Hakeem Shah, who nodded, satisfied with the selection.

"And the seventh?" Hakeem had an idea in mind.

"We are thinking of sending Khanaan with them! I know he is one of your commanders, but he can be trusted more than the rest, lest they deviate or waver in front of the innocents. We need your permission before listing him here, *Amir*," Ghulam said obediently.

"Khaakza." Hakeem Shah's voice resonated in the air.

Ghulam did not answer, at first. Finally, he spoke, his voice sounding strained. "Amir, we are aware of your close attachment with Khaakza and know well enough that this is a suicide mission—none of these recruits will make it back alive! The Pakistan army will not let them!"

"You know, Ghulam . . ." Hakeem Shah appeared behind him, bending over to observe him better, his eyes shining like steel. "Abraham's story has always fired my imagination as a religious militant. It is certainly a gripping one. 'Take your son, your only son, whom you love, to a certain mountain; there, the precious Ismael must be slain as an offering to the Creator.' And do you know what Abraham said? *Hineni*[30]—here I am!'" Hakeem turned around and stretched his arms wide. "And while

30 Hineni: Here I am in Hebrew

he raised his knife on the neck of Ismael, he was short changed with a ram and behold! It was a ram that was sacrificed—a ram!" Hakeem's smile widened.

It took Ghulam a moment to realize that he was talking about Khaakza—that for him, Khaakza was nothing more than that ram, whom he loved and fed like a beloved pet, only to one day be put under the knife. He was not Ismael! He could never be. None of them were. They would never put their own children through any of this. And from his perspective, it was accurate.

"My thought exactly, Ghulam!" Hakeem Shah seemed to overhear his thoughts as he took Ghulam inside from the terrace. And as they perched on the desk next to the blueprints of their plan, they howled with laughter, until their breath was short, and their ribs hurt.

"When should we inform them and start the training?" Ghulam inquired obediently once they'd regained control. Shah crawled into an armchair, exhausted by the sudden surge of amusement, fighting to restrain himself from laughing. He sauntered over to his glass and drank a few sips. With his fast metabolism, alcohol burnt off too fast for him to get drunk.

"Right now!" Hakeem Shah cried, feeling a chill of anticipation pass through him. The same evening, Ghulam ordered the seven recruits to assemble and join in Hakeem Shah's compound along with commander Khanaan and Master Qari. Ghulam gave them a brief overview of the operation and how they were supposed to attack the Army Public School and kill as many children as possible.

"Kill the children in a school, inside the army cantonment?" Khaakza inquired, incredulously.

"For Allah's sake! Yes, you must kill them all!" Qari responded in a controlled voice.

There was an uncomfortable silence in the room. "And this act in Allah's name will take me to Jannah, right?" Naqibullah whispered in Khaakza's ears. Khaakza stared at him, his eyes cautioning Naqibullah to remain quiet, lest he be flogged again.

The silence was penetrated by Hakeem Shah's commanding voice. "My children! The Army of Pakistan has been corrupted by the U.S., and has become a vassal for their desires. They have become infidels, and so have their children! Exterminating them is an act of justice. They have brought dishonor to our religion, killing our children in their assaults and air strikes. They *need* to feel our pain. Many pupils at the military-run institution are the offspring of army personnel. More than a thousand will be there when you attack. And by nightfall, most of them will be dead."

"And remember . . ." Hakeem Shah added, "this will not be easy! The devil will try to deter you from fulfilling your promise to Allah. He will use the children's cries, their blood and pain, their pleas, and innocent faces to dissuade you, to deter you from your path, but I warn you! Do not falter into disobedience, do not dare turn against Allah, lest you should perish too. They are the devil's disciples. If you look closely, you will see the devil in their eyes. They are the children of the soldiers, who have killed our people, taken away our livestock, our homes, our right to live! Fulfill the deed, for you are the righteous, the omnipotent, the infallible—you are Allah's executioners. Allah-hu Akbar!"

"Yes, *Amir*!" The camp resonated with cries of *Allah-hu Akbar, Allah-hu Akbar*! The men, led by Sadulayev, were amongst the Jamaat's ablest, battle-trained functionaries, except for Naqibullah, who was brought along merely as a decoy.

After a week of intense indoctrination lectures, the men were taken to a hill for target practice, some five kilometers away from their camp. There, another makeshift camp had been set up on a flat patch of land surrounded by deep depressions on either side. Small white canvas tents were erected for refuge from the sun's scorching heat. Sadulayev and Khaakzad were introduced as mission commanders, and took charge of the training, testing the skills and proficiency of the boys, giving them tips for improvement. They let them practice with AK-47's and smaller arms, testing them understanding of the suicide jacket and detonation mechanism.

They were also shown films on how to launch *fedayeen*[31] attacks, to understand the methodology.

The top leaders—Hakeem Shah, Khaanan, and Master Qari—had come to assess the progress of the training. Procedures were discussed, maps laid out, and entry points decided. Khaakzad was still skeptical as to how on earth a school surrounded by the army and within the cantonment could be attacked so expediently by armed terrorists and how they would not be intercepted on the way until he heard Khaanan speak about the role of "inside men" who were assisting them in their vicious plan of action including the intel on a center point in the school to kill as many children as possible.

On the other hand, Shah prompted Qari to set up an ideal stage for his post-attack speech, one that would elicit an ideal anti-religious response, as was desired of their mission. Master Qari took a few pictures of the boys alone, then alongside Hakeem Shah. Their loyalty was expressed as they held their guns proudly in front of a wide green cloth with the swords and kalma imprinted in white ink. The green symbolized the heavenly delights in the afterlife and the sword and the kalma in white ink was an emblem of jihad.

They used the reels sent to them to familiarize themselves

---

31 Fedayeent: suicide

further with the school and its vicinity, after which the boys were shown crudely shot video from a concealed camera.

On a huge board in the room were marked entry and exit points. Apart from the common deployment points, there was not expected to be many actual army personnel present in the neighborhood, on the day of the attack. They saw a small structure with a large gate on one side, across a busy road. The view then abruptly veered to the back side of the building. The school was the most vulnerable from the back end; the concrete-block walls had no vertical reinforcing and very little horizontal joint reinforcing from the back side. In addition, no seismic joints separated the school structure, creating low breaches that made it an easy infiltration point. The area on the backside was not only deserted, but fronted onto barren fields, much quieter than the front road entrance. They were shown a projected image of a hand-drawn map, enlarged, and dotted with scribbles, lines, crosses, large dots, and shading. Some areas within the school were numbered with names and details of those attack points.

"What better way than this to signal the arrival of the righteous in the very heart of the cantonment? Alhamdulillah. It will be our welcome note!" said Master Qari, his eyes moving over the excited faces of the boys. "Remember, do not give in to the children. You must show the might of the virtuous and the power of our message to the whole world. It is time for jihad. Hakeem and I will be in touch with you through our standard communication methods."

Vigorous training continued for the next few days. After that, the boys were taken back to the base camp, where they packed their bags and, after a quick meal, boarded a white van and followed Khanan and Ghulam, who guided them in a pilot vehicle. As they neared Dera Ismael Khan, Khaakza knew they were heading to a place close to Bannu. However, rather than taking the bridge road, their vans crossed to the other side of the city, towards Lakki Marwat District. After a long drive, they crossed a bridge in Kohat and entered Peshawar, soon arriving in the sparsely populated Adezai village. Passing a few small mud houses, they stopped outside a compound that housed a miniature mosque with tall minarets.

Since Peshawar sat near the restive areas along the Afghan border, it had become home to growing radicalism after the war on terror. The infiltration of the radical groups in the city suburbs was a common occurrence and the people of Peshawar had grown used to their lurking presence, demonstration of authority and reassertion of their militant credentials. Due to the long-standing friction between local militants, including between militants closely linked to Hakeem Shah, and the Pakistani state, a more hardline generation of radical operatives were now coming to the fore. This new breed appeared to be more ruthless and fanatical in perpetrating acts of terrorism.

The boys prayed there for over an hour, then rested the remainder of the night. The next day, they were introduced to other militant commanders operating in Peshawar, engaged to train the boys in intelligence gathering and telecommunication techniques. The expert's name was Abdullah, alias *The Hawk*, an expert in computer networks. The compound within held a sophisticated communications lab. They were also taught about online reconnaissance, surveillance, coding, and decoding of messages from the base camp, and given online intel about the school and the areas surrounding it.

Abdullah had brought along electronic gadgets, handheld devices, and phones that were registered under unknown male and female names, as well as laptops and radio sets. These were carefully set up in the lab. Two GPS handsets were handed out to the commanders. The training and plan had been worked out meticulously, much to Hakeem Shah's delight. A day before the attack, a few of the camp's local madrasah clerics visited them.

"Alhamdulillah, your sacrifice shall not go in vain," one announced proudly. "They deserve to languish in hell! Praise be to the Almighty and may Allah grant you paradise. Angels are waiting for you in heaven, and when you lay down your lives, your bodies will smell like perfume and you will shine like the moon itself," he said, his eyes scrutinizing.

They repeated the utterance, that their actions were for Allah; it echoed in Khaakza's mind as he prepared for the attack. He looked into the mirror as he put on his suicide vest, slinging the Kalashnikov over his shoulder, and fastening a machete to his belt. He gave one final stare at his cold face, his eyes meeting their reflection. His heart had grown icy and numb; the cloning process was powerful enough to make his own feelings inaccessible to him. Yet, he felt for a passing moment that something was not quite right or in place. He quickly discarded it on a whim. Working several weeks on something, only for it to be changed on a whim was not an option for Khaakzad. His faith went before him in all that he did. Even now, he was hiding behind that delusion, which was programmed and chipped in his subconscious reality from the age of seven. "*Ya Allah, for you*!" his voice announced before he covered his face with a shemagh.

ECLIPSE RISING

The emptiness of the early morning hours—a holy time—filled gradually with the sound of fajr azan. In Kaleemullah's household, the call to prayer was more welcomed than the desire to sleep, as he lay with Janat in the bosom of the predawn darkness. Janat woke first, followed by her husband; after performing their ablutions, she went ahead to Zufash's room. Her voice, floating out faintly from within: "Come, my son, it is fajr time, get up and perform your Salah. May Allah keep you safe and away from harm."

Janat's earnest invocations for her only son trailed off as he rubbed his eyes open and pulled his tiny frame up from the bed before falling back into the blankets. Well accustomed to this daily ritual, Janat smiled and gently pulled him up again.

As Zufash sat, raising heavy eyes, he saw through the open door of his room, across the narrow hallway with its dining table and chairs, to the bathroom door. There, the glass panel above the door showed the light burning inside the kitchen, and he knew that his mother had already started preparing his breakfast.

He washed his face, rinsed his mouth, irrigated his nostrils, and performed the rest of the ablution required of *wudu*. After being cleansed of the mysterious impurities of his sleep, he put on a fresh white jalabiya and cap and performed the fajr prayers on his prayer rug given to him by his father. Despite his daily use of the rug, the image of the Kaaba in Mecca seemed as vivid to him as on the first day he'd used it, praying next to his father. Following this, he sat cross legged on the tiny Persian mat, reciting the Quran while his father passed prayer beads absently through his fingers. Zufash's mind automatically began recounting the ninety-nine names of God, his lips whispering as he struggled to remember them all: The High, the Great, the Merciful, the Compassionate, the Guiding, the Powerful, the Avenger . . . until it was time for school.

Janat brought his egg *paratha*[32] and milk, in his favorite

---

32 Paratha: bread

marble-rimmed glass, on a round silver tray engraved with an image of the Holy House in Mecca Then she helped him change into his uniform, fixing his tie and brushing his hair softly so as not to tangle the tiny curls. Janat kissed his forehead, giving him a last, appraising look. Green pants and a white shirt freshly cleaned. A patterned tie above neatly polished shoes. He stood there, radiant, smiling back at his mother. A feeling came over her then, a strange fear, a spasm shooting through her stomach. He was so like a rare and endangered flower, she realized, innocent and pure amid a permissive and decadent world. She shunned the feeling, dismissing it as a mother's overprotective nature.

Zufash stood by the Mango tree in the veranda to say goodbye to his two loving pet parrots. Kaleemullah bought him a pair on his tenth birthday as they were quite talkative and play trained. They purred and squeaked when Zufash held them. After bidding them farewell, as Zufash walked out of the house, he looked over the murky road and brown grass rising out of a light morning fog. The trees appeared as shadowy structures suspended in air, oak, and poplars, now withered down to stalks. The remaining shaggy trees appeared like survivors of some terrible holocaust, the few clothed within a sea of naked and shaved forms. In the fog, he imagined the trees might never end, floating upward into eternity, limitless as beanstalks.

When they reached the end of their alley, he heard the revving of an engine, rising and falling, then cutting out. The air carried the stench of gasoline, a sign of a new day's beginning, a typical Monday morning in Peshawar as the roads quickly filled with traffic. The sky was a dreary, morbid grey, matching the feelings of those caught in the multitude of clogged streets all around the town, in the frigid December chill.

Crowds of pedestrians walked the edge of the streets, watching for an opportunity to cross. Students strolled under leafy shade trees, carrying school bags heavier than themselves, wearing warm woolen hats, gloves, and heavy jackets. Rickshaws tut-tutted past as the children waited for the buses, some crying as their mothers gently coaxed: "*Beta*,[33] it's going to be alright, you'll enjoy your friends at school. And when you return, I shall prepare for you a delicious meal."

The noise of cars and motorcyclists and rickshaws, of tanga wallas scooting past was deafening, a sea of activity, and within it, the delicious aroma of Asian breakfast delicacies floating on the air, of *halwa poori*, *lassi walla*, pungent curries, fried chicken, and sweetmeats, tempted passersby. The street hawkers, pedaling their wares. Little children, their backs and faces pressed against the doors and windscreen of the school bus, obscuring the driver's

---

33 Beta: my child

vision, to the annoyance of the parents frantically flapping their arms to flag down the bus. The Warsak road filled with little and big feet alike, all making their way to their school. Among the crowd was Janat, escorting Zufash, the boy eager to reach school, excited to meet his friends, wearing his green blazer against the cold. Janat set his mussed hair with her fingers, fixed his tie, and promised to wait for him outside the school gate.

"Amma will wait right here. You be a good boy, do not bother Miss Shafaq. Finish your snack, I made you *aalu paratha.*[34] There is also chocolate milk, your favorite." But Zufash already knew what his mother had made, for the bag carried the tantalizing scent of coriander and bread.

Janat bid him farewell, watching him slowly disappear into the thick crowd of students as they pushed toward the main doors. It was her habit to remain until Zufash was inside. Usually, he watched and waved, but today he only peered back, as Janat drifted on the sea of love, she bore for him. *Go in safety, my son,* Janat prayed, silently. *Fi Aman Allah.*[35]

---

34 Aalu Parahta: Bread with Potato stuffing inside.

35 Fi Aman Allah: In God's safety.

THE CULTIC RITUAL

The day began like any other for Zufash, though somehow felt different. He remembered saying goodbye to his mother, but for some reason did not avert his eyes and look away from her. Today, there was an ocean of love in her eyes and innumerable prayers on her lips. He wanted to run back and hug her again, but the school bell rang, and he made his way to class.

Today was December 16th, a special day. He was reciting on the stage for the first time, in the high school first-aid assembly. It was not a planned recital; he was only told a while back that there was an impromptu assembly in which he was required to recite. He had a beautiful, melodic voice, and his Islamiat teacher, Ms.

Sheikh had asked him to recite Surah Rehman at the beginning of the ceremony. He was in his English class when his name was announced over the P.A. He looked at his watch, realizing that he was nearly late.

"Oh, I forgot, the assembly will start in twenty minutes. Ms. Sheikh must be looking for me," Zufash said, raising his hand.

"Yes, what is the matter Zufash? Where are you being summoned?" Ms. Mehrooz asked him.

"Miss, I have to go to the auditorium, I am reciting on the stage today for the highschoolers." He inflated his little chest with pride.

"Ahh that is great news, Zufash! Well done, *beta*, it requires a lot of courage to stand up in front of an audience. Class, clap for Zufash and wish him luck."

The class boomed with applause and cheers, and Zufash felt elated. Thanking his classmates, he ran toward the auditorium where Ms. Sheikh was already waiting for him. "There you are *beta*, I was waiting for you. The students are settling down. Munawar has checked the microphone, and everything is okay. Are you nervous?" Ms. Sheikh asked, rubbing his cheek affectionately.

"A little, Miss, not so much," Zufash nodded slightly.

"Don't worry, my child. You will recite Allah's name. He will give you the courage and the strength, and you will be just fine. I will be standing right here," she said, pointing behind the curtains. "Once you finish, you come to me, okay?"

Zufash nodded his head obediently.

Soon, the hall was brimming with students and faculty chatting and laughing. The principal, Mrs. Khanum came on the stage then, asking everyone to be silent. The auditorium became peaceful. She then welcomed everyone to the assembly and instructed the students to show their best behavior while learning about first aid. "But first, I would like to call up Zufash Kaleem from Grade Five to recite a surah from the Quran before we begin."

Zufash made his way to the stage with trembling legs, nervous at such a big crowd. However, the sound of clapping combined with Ms. Sheikh's kind smile bolstered his spirits. He began his recitation with reverence in his voice.

"*Bismillahir Rahmanir Raheem! Ar-Rehman!*" (*In the name of God, who is the most merciful and kind! The Most Gracious Allah!*)

"Stop the assembly! Stop the assembly! We are under attack!" Munawar, the IT clerk, rushed inside as a flurry of gunfire sounded. He closed the door shut behind him. The shooting outside was suddenly accompanied by a shaking blast. One of the militants had blown himself up. Mrs. Khanum grabbed Zufash's hand and moved him away from the stage.

Sadulayev, half of his face covered, entered seconds later, and followed by Zawal and Naqibullah, each from different entrance points. They were all armed with AK-47s, rifles, and hand grenades.

"Anyone in the room whose parents are in the Army?" he bellowed sarcastically, then repeated the question three times.

The hall erupted in panic. Before anyone could move, Sadulayev grabbed Mrs. Sheikh by her hair, dragging her to the center of the stage. He cut a chunk of her hair with his knife, then poured kerosene oil on her and set her on fire. The children watched in horror as her screams echoed around the hall. Zufash's eyes filled with painful tears. Her loving face appeared in front of his eyes, as moments ago she told him to be courageous.

The children screamed and began to run toward the main door, which, surprisingly, was left open, unobstructed. Zufash was pushed from behind and fell to the ground, in between chairs, as other students piled on top of his back. The children poured out like running water, scattering as their screams grew louder, racing to save their lives . . . only to realize that they were trapped like a cork in the jug. For Abdul stood outside, waiting with a menacing smile. He shot them in a single file, one after the other.

Soon, the bodies of dead children blocked the entrance door, strewn all around, the cries of the wounded casting over the courtyard. Zufash heard the principal, Mrs. Khanum, scream, aghast at the barbarism on display, pleading with the attackers to leave the children alone as she shielded a group of them behind her.

"And what will you do to stop us? Who are they to you?" one of the men questioned harshly. He wore a long red beard.

"I am their mother!" Mrs. Khanum shouted, defensively. "They are all my children, and I will *not* let you harm them!" At this the man laughed contemptuously, as she stood before him, unarmed, carrying only the spirit of a lion. "Then, we will kill you first!" One of the men exclaimed, unrestrainedly.

Zufash watched as they first shot at her feet, killing one of the children just behind. Another shot to her stomach, another barely missing her head. She staggered forward, one arm reaching out to the children, grabbing at the air. Her head dropped, and Zufash thought she would collapse, but she looked up again, still ready to defend the children. One more bullet went through her shoulder, and she slowly sunk to the ground. A final bullet went into her head. It was Khaakza's. She hit the ground, face first, her hand still stretched out toward the children. Zufash squeezed his eyes shut, his heart racing, eyes filled with terrified tears as he thought of his parents, Janat and Kaleemullah. If only he could reach them, they could save him. If only this was nothing but a bad dream.

If only.

The bodies suffocated him, but he did not move. It seemed as if his ears would burst with the penetrating sound of the gunmen's cries of *Allah ho Akbar*' and the earth-shattering cries of the children as he watched blood pour out from the multiple holes in their soft bodies, holes made by hard steel bullets. Then, there came an ear-piercing blast, as another of the men blew himself up amongst a group of Grade Nine students. A carpet of destruction, smothering countless lives in that hall. The sky seemed to bleed terror, foam-like clouds of blood particles hanging in the air, small body parts strewn all around. And then it was quiet. Complete silence, with only the occasional groan or restrained whimper to break its crushing weight.

A few minutes passed, and once the auditorium had fallen silent, Zufash began to move the dead bodies off him. When he didn't see any gunmen, he stood up, jumping through a mess of chairs until he came to the small dressing room off the stage, where a group of students cowered in silence. Some were dead, some were shot in the legs, stomach, or heart, some spewed blood from their mouths and noses. The stench of it was everywhere, along with the smell of gunpowder. Zufash dropped in the corner, leaning his head onto his shoulder.

Moments later, he heard two men arguing in Pashto. He crawled forward and peered through the keyhole. The men, one slightly bigger in build and height, was shaking the collar of the other, smaller man, who could not have been older than sixteen. They both wore shalwar kameez, and their heads and faces were covered with black-colored shemaghs. The only thing visible was their eyes.

"Aye, *Khabeesa*! How many times should I have to tell you, aim for the head, not anywhere else? Don't you listen? One bullet, at this range, that's enough. One shot, and the pain and fear end. An empty body collapses to the ground. Come to your senses, Naqibullah—shoot to kill. Do not be a coward."

"Let go of me, Khaakza! Who took mercy on me that I should show mercy to them? They are nobody to me, privileged scum, and that's all! When the masters used to hit me and whip me, everyone would laugh. Today, they will writhe in pain, and *I* will laugh. They are the children of the infidels—what difference does it make to you? They will die anyway, just like I will die today. But they will burn in hell and me . . . I will go to Jannah . . .! Don't you remember what master Qari told us earlier?"

"Don't you remember, Kha…?"

Before Naqibullah could finish, Khaakza gave him a hard slap on the face. Naqibullah spat blood.

"Let me take you there, first," Khaakza came at him again, but Naqibullah raised his gun. Before it could get any worse, both were distracted as Zawal entered and opened fire from the doorway, killing the children who faced him. Soon, there was a pile of little bodies on the ground. "What are you two doing over here? Hurry up! Sadulayev is asking for you, Naqibullah. Amir has ordered another blast. Now it is your time to shine. We need to distract the army. Khaakzay! Check whoever is still alive here, kill them, and move out. We must cover the classes as well. Hurry! *Sama da*? "[36]

Khaakza gave a fleeting look over Naqibullah. Though it was the boy's time, somehow his death did not mean anything to Khaakza. In any case, he was better dead than alive. They all were. In Khaakzad's world, they were the living dead; prone to be sacrificed in the name of faith. Thus, any form of human association or emotional attachment was unnecessary.

Khaakza moved swiftly toward the mound of bodies. Whoever was injured, Khaakza shot them in the skull, unaware of Zufash's presence in the dressing room. Zufash turned away. He could not watch anymore. His heart was thudding so fast, it seemed it would burst out of his chest. But he had to warn his friends, who were likely still in their English class. He had two choices— either to hide where he was and wait for it to be over or go out or try to save his friends. Pausing for a moment, he made his choice.

He snuck out of the dressing room along with two other high-

---

36 Sama da: Pashto word for Okay

school students. They grabbed his hand and ran toward the back entrance of the auditorium that led to the primary school wing. There, they arrived in hell. There were bodies everywhere, white shirts tainted with blood. Bags, shoes, and books were strewn all around the wreckage. The floors shone a crimson red.

A bullet whizzed past their head as they made a turn into the corridor. Frantically, they kept running, turning down various hallways, as their pursuers gradually closed in on them. Then they stumbled, turning down yet another hallway, this one darker than the others. One boy was shot from behind. The other took Zufash and hid behind a pillar. Multiple bullets hit the pillar. Then there came a shuddering blast from the Admin Block, distracting the shooter.

"Abdul! Come over here, hurry! Naqibullah has blown himself up. We are running out of time, there are more children in the secondary wing. Come on!"

Abdul shot six more times, missing the pillar, and hitting the wall behind. Then, he left for the secondary wing. Zufash and the boy ran and hid in his grade-five class. There, Zufash's friends Safi and Haider rushed toward him, and they embraced. There were twenty other kids inside, along with Ms. Farnaz, the Arts teacher. Zufash had always liked her for her kind demeanor and her big, sparkling eyes. She had long hair and was in her mid-twenties.

She had barricaded the door and they all huddled in the center of the room, away from the glass windows.

"Keep reciting. Children, keep reciting. The army and police will come soon; they must be on their way. Ya Allah reham[37], have mercy on the children!" Ms. Farnaz implored in a choked whisper, silently praying to Allah while the children followed suit with quivering lips.

Soon, there came another blast. The gunfire became extremely loud before it tapered off. Zufash and his friends glanced through the class windows. Chunks of granite littered the corridors. Bodies were scattered, most unmoving. Suddenly, there was a loud thud. Zufash saw a Grade Four boy running toward their class. He had been shot multiple times already and was bleeding profusely. One of the bullets had gone through his chin. Zufash knew he wouldn't survive, but he could not see him die like this while he was still breathing. The boy collapsed near their classroom door. Zufash and Saif went out and dragged his body in; however, while doing so, they were noticed by Ressam, one of the terrorists.

"Oye! Stop right there, *odreka*[38]!" he cried, running toward them.

"Get under your desk—fast! Get under your desk!" Ms. Farnaz

---

37 Reham: mercy

38 Odreka: Stop there

cried. Some of the children cowered. Some stood confused and panicked. Ressam kicked the door open and stormed in, his gun at the ready. He was followed by Zawal and Abdul. The children began to cry and scream, but Zufash was so scared that he could not even utter a sound.

They were already shooting when Ms. Farnaz blocked their way. "Don't do this *wruna*,[39] I beg of you!" she cried. "They are children, innocent little children! They cannot even fight back, do not kill them—have mercy, for Allah's sake."

"We are doing this for Allah's sake. Move away now, let us do our work, move!" Ressam shoved her aside, but she resisted and blocked their way again.

"You are taking Allah's name in vain, beghairat. You are the devil's pawn. You cannot kill them! Not in front of me. I will not let you. Perhaps, your Allah is as dead as your conscience, but mine is alive. I am answerable to my Allah, who is watching your savagery right now, *bakhuda*.[40] He will avenge the innocent blood you are so ruthlessly spilling. This blood will rise and roar on the Day of Judgment, this blood will testify, and all the world will bear witness to Allah's justice. He will destroy you, skin you alive, bit by bit, you will burn in agony; your screams will be

---

39 Wruna: Brothers

40 Bakhuda: By God

perpetual. You have not only called upon his wrath, but you have also called upon *Him*, and He *will* come, make no mistake! Do not dare touch the children!" cried Ms. Farnaz.

"I said, get out of the way!" Zawal demanded in a hostile voice. "Over my dead body!" screamed Ms. Farnaz.

The fearlessness of her voice shook Zufash to the core. He felt like saluting her and Ms. Khan and all the children and teachers, for their courageousness and for standing up, but it had only aggravated the terrorists further.

"Cut her throat, spill her blood already—why are you wasting time?" Abdul roared, seizing her with a firm grip around the nape of her neck. He wanted to inflict pain. Pain that would always make her remember how much they hated her guts, her bravery, and the truthfulness in her voice. To quickly extinguish this woman who was as eager to die as they were to kill.

He pushed her toward Zawal, who grabbed her hair and wrenched back her head, causing her to cry out in pain as he shouted in her face. "Save them now! Where is your Allah, call him! Call him!"

He punched her in her lower back; she screamed, as burning fire engulfed her insides. Then he pushed her roughly to the ground.

"He is watching you—my Allah is watching!" She tried to swallow the cry in her voice; it came out only as a faint warble.

Zawal poured a liter bottle of lighter fluid over her head, shoulders, and upper body. Then he set her ablaze. Through the darkness of their hearts, her body blazed orange. The room crumbled to nothing but a shell, spitting flame as Ms. Farnaz burned.

"Run away," she cried out from behind the rising smoke and flames as her clothes melted and peeled away from her body. "Run my children, run—"

Zufash knew she was going to die and began to cry. Everyone was crying, but no one tried running away. There was no escape, as her screams shattered the air, her flesh sizzled, her big dove eyes scorched, her long beautiful hair crisped away, and her skin turned charred black in front of the children.

Zufash, numb in his horror, smelled her burning flesh as its black smoke billowed around the room. It held him, stunned. Sounds were muted as he beheld the horrific scene, his mind unable to comprehend. He heaved in a shuddering breath and muffled his cries with his hand, as the smoke of her threatened to choke him.

Then the men started spraying bullets. They shot his classmates in the head, in the chest, in their arms, legs, and stomach. Everyone was on the ground. Zufash was hiding under the desk with Saif, in the last row of the classroom, both boys shaking with fear as the deafening sounds of gunfire roared all around them.

"Be still Saif," Zufash whispered, swallowing, his mouth dry. But it was too late. Zufash saw the big black boots marching toward him. He heard their rhythmic beat across the floor, his death approaching. One of the men kicked at the desk, and Zufash's heart leapt into his mouth. He gasped and shut his eyes, drifting into his thoughts, into an image, a strange vision that flooded over his mind. He was at home, sitting under the tree, mangoes hanging from its boughs. He was recalling the names of Allah to his father, Kaleemullah; *the most Merciful, the Powerful, the Avenger . . .*

Then he felt it—as if a hot poker had been stuck through his chest, just to the right of center. It burned all the way through him. Suddenly, he couldn't breathe. He opened his eyes and saw blood spurting from the bullet hole in his chest. The burning moved up his arms and tightened his chest. His heart felt as if it were being wrenched and twisted. He opened his mouth to scream, but nothing came out.

His friend Saif was also hit with the bullets, though Zufash didn't know where. Nonetheless, he was still breathing. Zawal screamed to the other man, "Is that one dead?" and then Zufash heard bullets and more shots. He felt like he was staring directly at Death himself. Then they heard more gunfire, shots coming from outside. The sound distracted the men, and they ran outside.

The room was echoing with horrible cries of pain. Ms. Farnaz's charred body was lying near the teacher's desk, her purse and scarf still lying on the ground, now strewn with ash. The chalkboard, ironically, depicted a happy scene, of children playing outside the school, holding hands. This was what Ms. Farnaz had intended them to draw today.

He looked up at the date—December 16—and worried that if he dies today, his mother will never forget this day. All the mothers will never forget when innocent children like him lay sprawled like broken dolls, their joy stilled forever for coming to school...? Why are they hurting us? His little mind wandered, numb with fear and confusion. He was holding on to his school badge gripping it so tight in a fist his fingers felt like they would separate at the knuckles. It was impossible to describe the look in his eyes; His fear grew, got bigger, until there was just one thing left for him to do, and you better do it well, *Zufash.* He said to himself.

THE CONJUNCTION

The children's uneven breathing filtered quietly through the silence as the clock in the classroom chimed eleven. The only other sound's the wind, as it sighed mournfully through the line of trees that circled the school, as if lamenting the loss of innocence, of humanity. Zufash opened his eyes and turned his head to stare toward the glow of the morning light. It seemed so dark, and he could scarcely distinguish the window from the walls of his classroom. Tearful, he looked around. Everywhere lay lifeless faces he knew, faces he loved—old and new friends of his childhood, his faithful companions, his devoted teachers. He heard Haidar cry and whimper from the corner of the classroom, shot multiple times in his legs and stomach. Blood poured out of him as he hunched over his cell phone.

"*Amma,* please *Amma,* come and save me! Tell Baba to come and take me from here. All my friends are dead. I am in a lot of pain, *Amma*, it hurts . . . . . .it . . . hurts a lot *Amma*, please . . . tell Baba to save me, please *Amma*!" He coughed up blood. "I am very thirsty *Amma* . . . I don't want to die, I am so scared, hide me in your lap *Amma*."

Amma—the sound resonated in Zufash's mind, bringing his own mother's face to him as though out from a distant dream. "Be safe, my son," she had said. And why wouldn't he be? What could happen to him in a place like school, where children came to learn, laugh, and play together peacefully? Who would want to hurt children? It was the safest place on Earth, he'd always thought.

Zufash tried to reach out to Haidar, but the bullet in his heart caused him to retch gobs of blood before crumpling back to the ground. That was when he saw the man enter, the same man who was arguing with another in the hall. Then, Zufash knew it was the end.

Zawal went to the injured children as they cried on the floor of the classroom, writhing on the ground, begging for their mothers and fathers. He went to each one and asked them to recite the kalma, then shot them in the skull. He came to Haidar, who began crying frantically.

"He is coming, *Amma* . . . he is coming. He will kill me. I love you, *Amma*." Zawal aimed and fired at Haider, the bullet penetrating his skull, quieting him forever.

The phone remained in Haider's little hand, and Khaakzad overheard the despairing screams from the other end as he entered the classroom, the agony of that sound lost on him entirely as he stood there, cold as ice.

Gradually, they moved through the classroom, shooting each child in the head, until they finally reached the last row. Zufash gave a farewell look toward Saif, but his friend was already gone. At that point, Zufash couldn't hold back his tears any longer.

Zawal kicked a chair to clear his way and Zufash saw him, standing tall above him. Zawal gave a fleeting look down at his blood-soaked chest and mouth and asked him coldly:

"Recite the kalma, boy."

Zufash sat up as much as he could and met the man's gaze. "*Pehlay tum*!" (First, you!) Recite the kalma…!

Then and there, something broke inside Khaakza who also heard Zufash's reply. The distant echo was so potent that it rattled his very being, filling him with a surge of conscience. He slowly approached Zufash and their eyes met. He looked at the little boy glaring bravely back at him, daring him, daring death—like a fearless lion. A sudden sweat made tracks down his face, coursing through the dirt and dust. He remembered—a cloudy memory, like the dream of a dream, but he knew it was true. A story of a boy, lost in time. A shining sun he once knew, so much like this child, pure of heart—his father's pride, his mother's star—a true Wazir.

You should never fear death. Look it in the eye when it approaches. You are my son; you are a Pashtun.

The words reverberated in his head, as myriad images appeared before his eyes, drifting past as quickly as they came. His eyes and attentiveness came back to Zufash and he felt, as if he was staring into Bahadur's eyes, right before losing it all, to war and senseless violence. He grabbed his head with both hands.

"No . . . no . . . it cannot be!" Khaakzad cried out. He would not accept it. He was not wrong, he couldn't be. He was righteous. He was infallible. He was omnipotent, Allah's appointed executioner. These children, along with everyone else, were meant to stand before him and tremble. They would find no mercy with him. He was not capable of such feelings, of any feelings, for that matter. Mercy would be left to Allah. Khaakzad was meant to send them to Him, and thus earn his reward in the Hereafter. Wasn't that the lesson? Then why was he sweating, as he looked into the eyes of this child? He had put this armor of Allah to take his stand against the devil's evil schemes. But this triumph was not against his own flesh and blood or over the relentless onslaught from the forces of evil, but against children. Children? Little innocent children.

Courage mocked him, and he felt like nothing so much as vacant clay before the child.

"Khaakzad"—now he heard the irony behind his assumed identity and knew he could never defeat this boy. Not with fear, not with a gun, not even with death. But what else did he have?

The little boy had risen to a place Khaakzad could never reach. This was Allah's justice. He had lost to a little man. The shame, the disgrace . . . engulfed him. The realization expanded along the inner surface of his systematic molding, creating a visible crack.

He looked to the boy again, this time with an effort to find the devil within him; alas, all he saw was a child. A blameless and pure child of Allah. He could not bear that gaze—the pain and truth of it. Nor could he bear to remain any longer. Quickly, he aimed for the child's head. With quivering hands and a sweaty forehead, he placed his finger on the gun barrel, but he was unable to pull the trigger, his hands shivered like a tree in a hurricane.

"Khaakza, what are you thinking? Kill him, hurry!" Zawal snapped indignantly from behind, but Khaakza stood there, with his arm outstretched, the gun wedded to his shivering hand and his eyes on Zufash with an unholy guilt-ridden heart.

For a moment, Zufash saw his mother fretting over a minute scratch on his finger, placing the bandage over it while she kissed his face. He smiled at the thought, when Zawal sent the final bullet into him, detecting Khaakza's inaction. Zufash's lips released a last, whispered call. "M…aa…" that was cut off by a quick erupting scream from Khaakza.

"No….!" In a spiteful rage, he turned around and shot Zawal in the head, thrice.

Zawal's lifeless body crumpled to the ground. Khaakzad went to his knees beside Zufash and held him up, as if carrying the residual fragments of his own childhood; holding little Bahadur, today he died once more. Blood barely trickled from the wound as Zufash's little body rocked backwards in Khaakzad's arms; his eyes remained open, their light extinguished forevermore, his final thought that of his mother, a gentle smile frozen on his lips.

Now, his light was gone. Allah had finally spared his fragile body the unbearable pain. For Khaakzad, and those like him, the pain would go on. Khaakzad felt Zufash eyeing him still, calling him out as a pitiful, shattered wretch. His eyes would not let Khaakzad die without knowing that, without having full knowledge of his defeat. Of how complete and total it was.

Khaakzad's cheeks appeared hollow and flaccid, his eyes were full of wild incredulity as he held on to Zufash's lifeless body, his pulse ran slow knowing that his only chance of redemption was now gone. Khaakza looked around. He saw his former self, little Bahadur, in each one of the dead bodies. It was him who was dead—not them. Their lifeless faces staring back, accusing him, the question like a chorus in his mind, even in the deafening silence of the room. How many times will you die, how many times will you kill?

Why Why Why?

I did it for Allah, do you hear me? I did for Allah! His involuntary mind shouted its reply over the din, but even his conditioning could not repel the truth any longer. He screamed then, a tearing sound; it beat at the walls, casting over the bodies sprawled around him, filling the air so tightly he thought he might suffocate in it. Everywhere he looked, he saw the dead bodies of little children. He was alone, as alone as a man could be while still breathing, yet he could not escape Zufash's eyes. That gaze delved into the endless caverns of his mind, and he knew there could be no escape. All these years, all this training that he underwent along with the systematic indoctrination that was forcefully embedded in his system through torture and cruelty, to engage him and the likes of him in mindless killing under the pretext of spiritual warfare now demanded a rationale, a justifiable reason, but there was none.

His heart pounded, every pulse searing him as though with a hellish flame. The past personal connection and memories that he had eventually lost during years of mental assault started appearing, nebulously on the memory screen. He was painfully looking inwards, this time, with a self-conscious theater of memory, at the strata of brainwashing experiences carefully laid down in his own sedimentary layers. All the unsought feelings of rebellion, distrust, sadness and suffering of past years cropped up at once. It pierced his heart, each scene of killing, of torture, of mindless slaughter was like a site for an acupuncturist needle; it triggered a flow of physical and emotional pain that exceeded a thousand-fold, the scope of the point touched. The confluence of images as they assailed him, echoed the unwelcomed culpability. Helplessly, he convulsed, thrashing, his skull a ball of pure agony, filled to the point of bursting.

"No…! It cannot be!" His hoarse scream reverberated against the walls of the school as he ran out of the classroom, scrambling, almost falling, and careening aimlessly through the blood-soaked corridors.

Kill the children, kill the children! Khaakzad saw Master Qari across the hall now, his voice a temptation, breathing a devil's whisper. That was not Allah's voice. He could not find Allah anywhere, he realized, and knew he no longer needed to search for truth in his existence thus far, for it was nowhere to be found.

Khaakzad could not face himself. He fell on the ground, screaming miserably.

"Confirm your position." Voices on the other side of the transistor shouted again: "Confirm your position!"

In forty-five minutes of holding the power, his world had changed. The army had now entered the school premises. Khaakzad heard the incessant firing from the other end of the building. He could no longer respond. He could no longer be a part of whatever this was. He flung the transistor onto the floor, and it smashed into pieces. He grabbed his heart, which ached mercilessly. "Oh, the pain, I must get rid of the pain." He glanced down at his gun's huge barrel, black and gleaming, as his hand clenched his heart. Khaak had never feared death. Instead, it was life he feared. He could no longer face its truths, those realities. With one final bawl that echoed into eternity, he shot himself, bleeding to death from a bullet wound to the heart. That pain had finally ended, as did Khaakzad/Bahadur's life, draining into the sands of time.

MILLS OF GOD

Children held a special place in most Pakistanis' hearts; they were considered an *amanat*, a trust from God, as well as a *barakah*, a blessing from God. And yet, on this day, that trust was breached. For a single, endless moment, there was silence in Peshawar, as a city of fearless hearts stood frozen in disbelief.

Then, the wailing and screaming began…

Warsak Road was now littered with dead and dismembered bodies that had been carried out from the rubble on doors, boards, and benches. Small headless bodies and random body parts created a vision of hell. The horrific darkness of the scene consumed them all and could be heard in the tone of the cries that slipped from the quivering lips of the families who had gathered, praying their children were not among the dead. Other bodies had been laid on the side of the dusty road and were covered with what little tarpaulin or plastic sheeting could be found. When those materials ran out, quilts, curtains, and sheets from a nearby draper took their place.

A small boy, no more than six years old, sat motionless amid the awful stench of burning bodies—he did not cry, though the leg that had been blown from his innocent body was later found inside the school, the shoe still on.

Military vehicles and officers strategically surrounded the site. Several of the army officers, Edhi crew, and paramedics, their uniforms crusted with blood and dust, broke down crying. Many of the small bodies they had carried out of the rubble were already dead.

Trails of bloody footprints crisscrossed the debris-littered playground. Pools of blood, both inside and outside the school building, oozed over the small, wooden desks inside. A cacophony of electric saws, sirens, and rickshaws mingled with the sobbing voices.

Towels, coats, and handkerchiefs became makeshift bandages for the wounded. Ambulances swung around the narrow turn in the road and transported the injured to Lady Reading Hospital. But there were too many of them. Even with extra staff and facilities, the hospital could not cope with the scale of the carnage. The road to the hospital was partially blocked, filled with those desperate for news about their children and loved ones, as well as by others eager to assist, to give support, blood, whatever they had to offer.

From the back windows of receding ambulances, the wounded children stared out blankly, their parents and loved ones providing the only human sounds: screams of unimaginable grief, cutting through the deep chasm of the encroaching night.

The air was gray with diesel fumes, wafting through the stench. An old man in his carpet slippers shuffled by with the help of two sticks, reaching for the school gate, asking after his son in labored breaths. On the far side of the road, a woman with a little girl by her side implored a guard, "I beg you, please find my son, his name is Murtaza . . . he is in grade three. His father dropped him to school this morning, now I cannot find him. Please! I beg you, for Allah's sake, find my son!"

Kaleemullah had been at his office on University Road when militants had stormed the Army Public School. He'd left immediately, requesting a colleague to drop him to the school on his motorbike. University Road was completely closed off; there was no space for even a bike to pass, and so he remained stuck in traffic, trying to make his way through. At the same time, Janat was making lunch for Zufash at that time when she saw the news on TV. The food tray fell from her hands as she turned and ran, barefooted, her black shawl falling behind her. Their house was a lot closer to the school, so she reached before Kaleemulah.

Soon after, she'd called him to say that she was in Defence Park, looking for Zufash among the survivors, and that she could not find him there. She rushed back to the school, but the army officers would not let her through. "We cannot let you through, Bibi, the evacuation team is in there. You should look for your son in the ambulances or at the hospitals."

And so, she ran, spinning back and forth as she circled the school in wild patterns, screaming silently in loss and fury. "My son!" she cried to anyone who would listen. "My son! Have you seen my son, Zufash?" No one had seen him. She felt helpless and weak. In that moment, she remembered Allah, what she had read in the Holy Scripture only the day before. Was that a sign? She could not tell. She imagined Hajar's[41] pain, who'd traveled back and forth between the hills Safa and Marwa seven times in the scorching heat with whatever energy was left in her body, as she breastfed her baby Ismael, searching for civilization, hoping,

---

41 Hajar: or Hajirah (her name comes as Hagar in the Bible) – wife of Ibrahim (as) and mother of Ismail (as) – to be remembered for all times to come. Her "Sunnah" is an integral part of an obligatory pillar of Islam – the Hajj.

and believing in Allah and His mercy. Janat looked up then, with tears in her eyes, and silently prayed to Allah.

O Rabbi, please have mercy on me. I feel Bibi Hajar's pain today. Her heart must have broken at the sight of her son dying before her eyes. She was a righteous and pious woman, but I am a sinner, an ordinary woman, and cannot fathom the pain of losing my son. I do not have the heart to bear it, Ya Allah. Have mercy, please, return my Zufash safe and sound. The prayer comforted her and gave her strength. Then, Kaleemullah called her again. He would go to the hospital to look for Zufash, as someone had seen him there.

"They have seen Zufash—my Zufash?" She was overjoyed and thought she might prostrate herself right then and there, in thanks to Allah Almighty. The very thought awakened a renewed hope in her heart.

While Janat went back home to wait for Zufash, Kaleemullah sought him out at the Combined Military Hospital (CMH). There, as he looked under each of the white sheets covering the dead; each time, however, as his hands shook, he found a different child instead, feeling both relief and misery at once. All of them looked like Zufash to him. Each of them, the apple of their parents' eyes. He did not find Zufash there, so, tired and devastated, he rushed to Lady Reading Hospital (LRH).

For several hours he searched at LRH, finally finding his boy's body amongst the unidentified corpses, for Zufash's school identity card had fallen away when he was shot. Kaleemullah finally saw the face he sought, the face he had kissed and caressed so many times, now lying on the slab, black and blue, filled with wounds but no longer with life. His only son, his life's asset, his bright little star . . . gone. Kaleemullah fell to his knees, shattered and heartbroken. He tried to speak, but his voice only croaked as he closed his mouth, opened it, and closed it again. Standing away, he wiped his face with his sleeve, as a silent world of storms erupted inside him, in the fading light of his son's last day, staring at his ten-year-old boy's dead body.

More people arrived in search of their loved ones, stunned by the scene of blood-soaked pavement. Those who found their children alive were kneeling in *sujood*,[42] kissing, and holding on to their children and thanking Allah Almighty while others wept bitterly for their loss.

This tragedy of unimaginable proportion rendered their very spirits immobile as though they had been imprisoned by an evil enchanter. Mothers, dazed with grief, wandered aimlessly through the streets as a pall of thick, black smoke rose from the carnage and disappeared into the December clouds, a sight nearly

---

42 Sujood: kneeling while praying

impossible to fathom.

A trail of blood led up the steps of the hospital. The walls, floors, sinks, toilets—no surface had been spared the stain of blood. Injured children were laid out on mattresses in the corridors, and the scene in the halls of the hospital was perhaps worse than that of Warsak Road—if such a thing were possible. Doctors and nurses, their faces distorted with devastation, coped as courageously as possible, many drifting into shadowy corners to weep quietly before returning to their duties. One father, his white singlet stained with blood, sat on the floor cradling the body of his injured daughter as another relative held a drip above her. Another two children arrived—one a seven-year-old boy with shrapnel lodged in his body: the other already gone.

Hospital workers struggled to compile a list of the deceased, but the details were few and hard to come by. Clearly, the death toll numbered in the hundreds, most of them children. The number of injured remained unclear as well. The hospital staff carefully sifted and separated the dead from the injured, weeping softly along with Peshawar itself—indeed, all of Pakistan— inconsolably, a nation diminished by tragedy, drowning in her tears.

***

The next day was icy and tempestuous. It had been raining since fajr and a very cold biting wind was blowing, chilling everyone to the bone. It was around eight in the morning when Colonel Hamid along with two army officers arrived at the Kareems' residence. Hamid went to the front door and knocked. An elderly woman received the officers, each clad in stiff khaki uniforms. Before she allowed the three men into the house, she asked them to wait, while she returned inside to prostrate before Allah in the prayer room. When she returned, Colonel Hamid stepped forward, taking her hand.

"Mrs. Kareem, congratulations! Along with five other soldiers, your son and our friend, Captain Feroz Kareem, have embraced martyrdom, while saving the lives of hundreds of children. We were still planning our incursion strategy. Yet, once he heard of the attack, Captain Feroz went in alone to intercept the terrorists. His firing gave an impression of full army infiltration to the terrorists. Due to him, they panicked, and hundreds of lives were saved. You should be proud of Feroz."

The officers handed across his cap, as well as the flag that had wrapped his body. She received it with both hands, her body trembling, her eyes filled with tears.

"Alhamdulillah, my son, it is more than an honor. His father would be equally proud. Feroz fulfilled his promise today. I have surrendered both my husband and my son to my land. As my husband used to say, 'I will fight to the last man and the last round.' He could not have had a better successor than his son Feroz. May Allah accept their sacrifice and give them the highest rank in the Hereafter."

His funeral along with other martyred soldiers was attended by a host of dignitaries and citizens. Feroz's mother and the rest had hoped that their son would be married one day, that they would have a wife and children, and that they might see another generation thrive and grow. The band would play merry wedding songs, and the *shehnai*[43] would bless the auspicious day. Now, however, all the mothers heard was the sound of the gun salutes, the national anthem played as their sons' bodies clad in blood-stained uniforms descended into the earth. In the days following the colonels' visit, the Chief of Army Staff had also visited Feroz's home, commending the young officer's courage.

"I hope you will bear this loss with courage and fortitude. He confronted the terrorists alone. Had he not, many more lives might have been lost. I salute your son's courage and his will to serve his country. The government of Pakistan has decided to honor him with Tamgha-e-Shujaat; a gallantry award in recognition of his

43 Shenai: wedding music instrumental

bravery and sacrifice. Had he returned safely, he would be sitting at my post, in due time. I take his death as a personal loss."

Mrs. Kaleem kept Feroz's badge of honor on a table in his room before a picture in which he posed contentedly with his parents. Every morning, she bowed her head in prayer, looking to his face in the image, kissing the picture, knowing that he now lived in communion with the land he held sacred. The soil in which he was buried had embraced him like a mother. Its winds, whether they blew hot or cold, would always remind him of her motherly caresses. Everything about this land—its fragrances, its diversity, its terrain— reminded her that her son had lived, along with the rest who sacrificed their lives for a purpose and so she celebrated his existence just as she celebrated her own.

A scent of camphor and rose petals rose from out of the martyred children's graves. By contrast, Khaakzad and his companions were not accorded even a small clump of earth in which to rest, only a single large hole—a pit— into which their bodies lay piled and strewn like so much garbage. No ritual bath was given, no funeral prayers spoken, as none knew what religion it was that he and the rest followed.

While Khaakza's body was being dragged toward his final resting place, clouds of dust blew like curses, casting across the mound. Grains of sand, driving deep into his hair and eyes, nostrils, mouth, and throat. Grit filled the wells of his ears, and coated his skin, crusting his eye lashes. Under the blood-red sun, his defiled body was discarded; along with the rest of the terrorists—the forsaken, laid side by side—all hatred forgotten in their unified eternity of decay.

As Khaakza's corpse rotted, crumbled, and withered to dust, his soul was also cremated, along with his impurities, in the court of Almighty God. His journey to becoming Khaakzad— dust to ashes—had now come full circle.

THE NOBLE SACRIFICE

Kaleemullah entered the darkened room to find his wife sitting up in her brass bed, her head bound in a white shawl, a braid of black hair falling over one shoulder.

"Janat… it's time," Kaleemullah announced in a weak voice.

Minutes passed in silence, but Janat made no reply. Eventually, she staggered up to stare at her son's kafan[44]-wrapped body on the charpai. Kaleemullah wanted his son to be buried in his uniform like the rest of the children as Zufash was a martyr. However, considering Janat's deteriorating mental state, he let her prepare him one last time, for his final resting place and did not create a

44 Kafan: burial shroud

scene. She had not allowed anyone else to give Zufash the funeral bath; she had done it all by herself. No one dared say anything, for it was her prerogative, her last homage to her son. She alone removed his blood-stained clothes, then washed her son's body with camphor-scented zam-zam water. His head needed to be wrapped in numerous bandages, as the bullet had driven through his skull, emerging from a hole in the center of his forehead. Janat imagined him in that moment, blood trickling down over his eyes, along his nose, into his mouth . . . alone and scared, searching for her, craving her embrace. Had he called out to her as he took his last wisps of breath? "*Ammi*"[45]

She alone carefully washed his right arm and hand, twice; then the left, then the rest of his body, ending at his feet. While wiping his body clean, she rubbed her hand gently over the bullet-hole that had pierced his chest, as if trying to spare him any further pain. As if Zufash might cry out if she were to press any harder.

Wrapping a thread around his tiny toes, she tied his feet together, recalling how he'd kicked in her stomach. She had loved feeling him move inside her despite the discomfort.

Janat wanted to squeeze his little boy against her chest and never let go. "I'm here now, my son," she intoned softly. "With you. I won't let anyone come near you now." But he made no reply.

45Ammi: mother

Her irrepressible Zufash, with his plum cheeks, button nose, and deeply curious brown eyes, was silent.

She looked at his kafan-wrapped body and imagined blood pouring out of the bullet holes like water rushing through newly opened tributaries, turning his shroud scarlet red, as if it were her own blood coursing through her veins and into his, gushing out, a widening flow of life, warm and beckoning, soaking the clean white sheets of her bed. Janat journeyed down the memory lane where time in the present truly came to a standstill.

"Patience. Patience, Gul Bibi." That was all she heard, in her agony and desperation.

Patience.

It was a quiet morning, in a village like all the others, small and quiet, nuzzled in the wide green valley of Mansehra, as twenty two-year old Janat whimpered against the stinging pains of labor. Her husband, Kaleemullah, rushed outside to bring in his mother-in-law, along with Janat's sisters.

When the time drew near, Kaleemullah brought Janat to her father's house, so she could be better taken care of by her own mother, for Kaleemullah had no womenfolk in his house back in Peshawar. The advent of the child was to be kept a secret for as long as possible, per the custom, and thus Janat was kept secluded. Only the midwife and her own mother and sisters were allowed to attend to her.

Taking her to the hospital or clinic was not an option. No doctor or medication of any kind was allowed, also per the custom. The women, whispering quietly, went in and out of the darkened room, bringing cups of cool water and strips of clean cloth. Kaleemullah kept himself well away, leaving to pray at the mosque while Janat remained behind a locked door, breathing deeply against a pain like hot knives, one that spread from the lowest part of her belly to the very tips of her fingers.

She tried humming to calm against the pains and spasms. The room was hot, but peaceful, its walls white and clean, a few squares of sunshine falling across the simple mattress on the floor. She breathed. Janat wished to be by the sea. She would sit on its shores and let her pain drift out into the water . . .

She fumbled for the birthing ropes they had tied to the rafters, gasping as another pain ripped through her, gripping so tightly her knuckles turned white. Then the pain subsided, and she exhaled. The spasms were coming more quickly now. She whimpered, afraid. No one had ever told her just how much it would hurt.

Then it was over, and she heard the first bleating cry of her love seed. The midwife checked the baby over silently, then bathed him before Janat was able to hold him in her arms for the first time. A son. He rooted with his little mouth, searching for food, so she held him to her breast until he found her, and finally latched on. She nursed him for a long time, and when he was satisfied, she held him out in front of her. He opened his eyes, then, and looked at her—a fragile and bright creature, soft and new. She kissed him all over his face, marveling at his tiny body, his miniature hands, and feet. Zufash stilled under her gentle touch, grabbing her finger tightly, looking up at his mother, fascinated by her voice, by the soothing words she spoke.

Janat locked that gaze in her heart forever—his eyes, his face, and his implicit trust. Then, she and her newborn son lay curled together for hours, feeding and sleeping. She stared at her baby's perfect face for so long, as he slept, as she would for all his life. . .

* * *

As she did now in his white burial kafan, Zufash entered his eternal sleep when nothing could rouse him, not even his mother.

Sleeping so peacefully, she thought, running her fingers through his hair. She craved for him to wake, craved to hold him again, to be immersed in his presence and simply let the rest of the world fall away from them both. She wanted to hide him, keep him locked up somewhere inside of her, away from harm, from this world and its darkness.

"It's time." Kaleemullah's voice brought her back to reality.

Time for what, Kaleemullah? she thought absently. *Don't you see my son is sleeping?*

"Let him rest," Janat shushed, as if his voice could wake Zufash. "See, Kaleemullah, is he not as radiant as the sun? I dressed him in his army uniform, under the shroud. I don't like this white, you know, it's just so plain. So, I dressed him in his favorite costume—and look! He's wearing the cap too, with the *chand sitara.*[46] You know how upset he'll be if I don't let him wear it. He loves it, my son, *mera chanda!*[47] Go now, let him rest! You go, let me lie beside him." She lay close but didn't feel his warm breath on her face. Nor would she, ever again.

Kaleemullah fidgeted, looking helplessly over his wife. Her face, still so innocent and trusting, had lost its youthful glow through time and hardship. Her eyes had become sunken over the thirty-two-years of domestic drudgery, her skin hardened and lined like leather. The geometry of her jaw had softened, becoming sallow. Her voice was low and withdrawn. And yet, she went about her duties without argument or effort, only acceptance, respect, and patience. And what had he done? He could not protect the one person she cared for most, the boy she wished only to raise and

---

46 Chand sitara: moon and star

47 Mera Chanda: my moon

love, and it shattered his heart to see Janat clutching at their son's dead body. He struggled to keep himself from screaming at the agony of it. Zufash was his son, too—his only son. Found again, among the scores of other dead children, in a search so unnerving he had thought he might collapse with each step he had taken.

His world had ended that day; now, he watched Janat curled up against him—Zufash, in his white shroud with the army uniform underneath, he watched Janat's world collapsing as well. Ever since he had brought Zufash's dead body home, Janat had not shed a single tear. She did not cry at his blood-stained clothes, or as she gave him the funeral bath. Even now, when it was time to go, to deliver his boy into the ground. Kaleemullah folded his hands over his upper abdomen, his face turned away from her so she wouldn't see his silent tear. His voice cut the eerie silence like a blade.

"Gul, get up!" he called to her. "Our son has died a devout Muslim, unafraid and untouched by death. He is a martyr now; he has given up his life for his land and his country. He will be welcomed into paradise by Allah Almighty and his prophet Mohammad (peace be upon him). Grieving only denies Allah's divine will. Your cries will only cause the enemy to rejoice in the death of your son. Have patience and say your farewell. We must go now, before the sun sets." The words came out, half broken as his vision got swamped with Zufash's innocent memories.

He felt weak in his knees as Zufash's voice calling out to him reached a crescendo, an orchestra of insistent sound that threatened to tear his mind apart. It crashed against him, in multiple waves before finally receding.

"No, Kaleemullah," she replied softly. "Soon, he will wake up and look for me, he will call me. Amma! He will call me Amma, and you all will see, my Zufash is not dead, he is not dead." Janat hugged her dead son's chest and clung onto it, rocking slowly.

Kaleemullah called to Janat's sisters to remove her, knowing she would never let go. It was as though her own life depended upon that embrace. Gently, the women embraced her and held her against the furor of her cries and her pleas. Then, the grieving noises grew, emotions exploding as the charpai emerged, the deathly essence of roses filling the sorrowful air.

Zufash's body was lifted in the air, floating over hundreds of heads, and disappeared. The high-pitched wailing of the women's cries, their tear-filled, weathered eyes trailing the funeral procession, screaming so loud that it was as though Allah himself had been lost.

Kaleemullah stopped them with a single, scathing glare. The caterwauling ended as quickly as if it had been cut with a blade, replaced by the eerie moan of a stiff wind. Like swaying kites, they followed behind Zufash's body. As he walked, Kaleemullah lowered his gaze, to hide his contempt for the women making the offensive noise. The whole community had gathered for the children's funerals. There was one every few hours. Everyone was devastated. The woman's loud grieving and bleating expression of grief was not welcome here. Even though loud wailing was customary among Pashtun women, Kaleemullah never really appreciated it when a woman's voice crossed the four walls of his house. It was against the Pashtun culture, and he considered it shameful.

Janat unceremoniously forced a path between the mourning relatives, parting the group to see Zufash, but he was already out of reach. The door of the house shut her in with the rest of the women. As a cultural and religious restraint, women were not allowed to escort men in the burial procession to the graveyard. The virtue of following the bier was basically for men alone. Prophet Mohammad (peace be upon him) prohibited women to participate because they were too emotional when it came to matters such as the death of their loved ones. For that reason, Janat and the rest of the female relatives were instructed to stay within the confines of the house and mourn. But over the walls that separated women from men, cries mingled and broke this segregation. She still heard the shuffling feet, heard a man shout "*kalma e shahadat.*" She imagined Zufash's funeral bier passing on from shoulder to shoulder. It must be the heaviest *chaarpayi*, carrying her ten-year-old. She felt those feet trampling her heart as their sound fell away. "*La ilaha illallah muhammadur rasulullah*" hummed in the air.

Janat stood at the edge of the veranda, staring at the door. But her eyes saw only the past. The veranda had become a blank canvas, flashing pictures before her eyes. She saw herself bringing Zufash home as an infant, held in the nook of her arm, holding him close to keep him warm. She saw herself walking restlessly back and forth in the night air, carrying him, singing a lullaby when he had a fever. She saw herself pushing his scooter while he giggled and laughed, saw him playing in the veranda, sucking on ice lollies and sugar cubes. She saw him reciting on his prayer beads or reading the Koran with her on the *charpai* until it was time for Prayers.

She saw him entering the gate in his sparkling white and green uniform, rushing to the kitchen for a hug. She saw herself feeding him with her hands. She heard him call out to her, "Ammi, Ammi Jan!" and his sweet voice echoed in her mind.

The vegetable tray fell from her hands, and the loud noise of it broke her out of her reverie; now, all she heard were the mourners' cries; all she felt were the hands of the other women, shaking her back into the present. Looking back over the veranda, she saw

Zufash's blood-stained school bag, still lying in a corner. It had his name on it. She imagined the slab on the grave, beneath which he would lie forevermore, buried under tons of earth. She rushed to grab hold of his bag, then fainted.

Kaleemullah could hear the cleric chanting *surahs* from the Koran into a microphone. His words reverberated through the town, and after each round of prayers, groups of mourners lined up to condole the bereaved fathers before walking out of one door and into another. The verses took him back to his own son's graveside, and the bitter wind coming down the mountains made his wet eyes sting as he carried his beloved son to an early grave. He remembered carrying him to the zoo, or to the playground, or to the market. Zufash loved being carried and cuddled, his little arms gently reaching around Kaleemullah's neck, when he would rest his chin on his father's head. Never once had his boy seemed heavy—until now. It was the heaviest coffin he'd ever have to bear, one that would break his back and cripple him for life.

The gravedigger began a mournful dirge. Then voices rose into the clear air, rising and falling in eerie counterpoint to the constant wind. Fine dust blew into his face as he positioned his son's body over the open grave and began lowering it down. Kaleemullah clenched his jaw as it disappeared into the yawning hole. He set his back teeth as his son's corpse settled into its earthen cradle.

The cleric's droning words of prayer drifted past him. All he could think about was holding Zufash's bullet-riddled body. No one had lifted a finger to help Zufash or ease his pain, and Kaleemullah's hands balled into fists at the thought. He could still smell the warm blood mixing with the dust. He tossed the first shovelful of sand into the grave. Mourners followed and began filling the grave. They used their hands, as well as shovels, buckets, and trowels.

Kaleemullah fully covered his son with shovelfuls of the crumbling Pakistani soil from which he'd struggled to eke his living.

He made sure the earth was not packed too tightly, for Zufash needed to be able to sit up when the time came for him to undergo the angels' questioning. Kaleemullah had no doubt his son would answer each question correctly and earn his swift passage into paradise. His body would then join his soul when Allah called all true Muslims home on the Day of Resurrection. The crowd of mourners ended the final dirge as he finished; then, one by one, left the graveside as Kaleemullah requested to be left alone. He knelt next to the grave and laid a hand on the mounded soil, staring at it with red-rimmed eyes, frozen in time. He knew that even if Zufash's mortal body was beneath the ground now, he would still hear his father.

"Thank you, my son, for making me a martyr's father . . .

Alhumdulillah - May Allah bestow his blessings upon you! I have resigned to Allah's will and have given my own blood, my most precious asset to Him and to my land. O Allah! I ask for your forgiveness and pray for Your support. Help me accept my son's fate, help me in overcoming my grief, this separation gnawing at me from within. I take my refuge in You, Ya-Allah! Have mercy! Zufash . . . O my Zufash, my beloved son!"

He threw himself on Zufash's grave and wept bitterly. He was a proud old man, a strong Pashtun, not sure how to speak of his grief, certainly not around people. He had held himself together all this time, perhaps to protect himself from the embarrassment of breaking down, but he didn't care anymore. He was mourning the death of his little Zufash, and the tears from his worn eyes flooded Allah's Arsh[48] in the seven heavens.

***

Along a row of nondescript houses, the floral, colorful curtains hanging at their main gates the only distinction between them was Kaleemullah's humble abode in Gul-e-Bahar. His house stood apart by virtue of the small emblem of the Pakistan army that adorned its entrance. The emblem bore his name and stated that

---

48 Al-Arsh: Arabic word for God's Throne

he was a patriot. The street was crowded now, tight, and airless, surrounded by plaster, scaffolding, bricks, and dust. The sun had nearly fallen behind the hills, and dusk tinted the sky pink and purple. A few blocks away, from the Haji Yaghoub Mosque, the mullah bellowed azan, calling for the faithful to unroll their rugs and bow their heads west in prayer. Electricity poles from Khyber Bazaar, Qissa Khwani, Misgaran Bazaar, Chowk Yadgar, and Bazaar Kalan—all the way to the interior of the city—were plastered with funeral announcements. Thunderheads rolled in, painting the sky iron gray. Within minutes, sheets of rain began to fall, bringing the swelling hiss of water. Slithering beads of rain sluiced down the windows of the Kaleemullah residence.

Friends and kinfolk arrived in droves to mourn the death of Zufash and the rest of the martyred children. As the winter sun settled into shadows, Kaleemullah nodded at the visitors, lifting his hands in silent prayer at each one who came to condole his son's death. The men's sitting was in the large veranda of the house, covered with Afghan rugs and thin mattresses placed in parallel lines. They filed onto the veranda, leaving their shoes at the entrance, and sat cross legged on the mattresses. They were mostly reciting verses quietly followed by inaudible grief burdened whispers in Kaleemullah's ears.

"Your son is a martyr as Allah has granted him the highest

honor as a Muslim, Kaleemullah! Be patient, my friend."

Kaleemallah drew his courage from their statements as he nodded and raised his hands to praise Allah.

"By Allah, I feel that our Lord is pleased with me, because I am offering something [my son] for Him. I ask Allah to give him the reward of a Martyr. Allah willing, he will be with the prophets, the Martyrs, and the righteous. I greet all the people who came today. It's true that there's nothing more precious than children, but for the sake of Allah – what is precious becomes inexpensive."

"Yes, Kaleemullah! But children are the apple of their parent's eyes. This is a difficult time, my friend. For you, for Janat and all of us. The whole country is mourning this innocent loss of lives. Curse these animals, they had no heart, no mercy! Our beloved city is bleeding! Do you remember the good old days, my friend?" His friend Gulwali rubbed his shoulders gently to soothe his best friend's grief-stricken body.

As the night faded, a grief-stricken Kaleemullah went to sit next to his son's grave. As he was leaving, he saw his brother's daughter trying to feed Zufash's pet parrots, but they refused to eat or speak. Walking through the neighborhood, he heard groans and muttered prayers all around him. He shook hands with people, receiving and passing condolences in turn, as he marched dejectedly toward his son's final resting place.

Peshawar was in deep mourning. The streets wore a deserted look, with most parts of the city, including business districts and markets, closed in mourning. Echoing with cries, the last rites of children who had died in the savage attack had been ongoing since the grisly attack. None of the people were trained to endure the violence that surrounded them. Blood running in the streets; blood drying on corpses strewn here and there, in some places piled up on top of one another . . . Death, and more death—all of it in prime time. Still, the natives somehow were trying to find life and hope amid all the destruction and fear. And perhaps that made Peshawar gruesomely fascinating because life went on despite the onslaught, and because the city, in its decline and decay, nevertheless remained a city.

Death was predetermined by Allah, meant to be accepted without condition. But Kaleemullah knew he could never accept Zufash's death. He could never move on, even if he wanted to believe he had. The past claws its way out. His son had died unnaturally, shedding his life's blood into the soil of their homeland while the perpetrators stood by and watched. The brooding stole his calm, for he knew now, as father to a lost son, what manner of fear lurked across the desolate mountains.

May Allah protect the innocent and my land. The silent prayer left the peripheries of his quivering lips with much pride and emotion, for he knew what this land meant to him and how much his ancestors had sacrificed for Pakistan. He shared with them the same blood, an interwoven past which began in the ancient subcontinent, then spilled wide across the borders. Their lives, pasts, hopes, dreams, identities, interpersonal relationships—everything—was shaped by what seemed like just another event in history. The disruption, lasting only a few months, had managed to fracture their entire existence. The trauma of leaving dead family members behind never left him or his family.

BARZAKH (INTERSPACE)

Almost one year had passed. No one who was at the Army Public School in Peshawar on December 16, 2014, was able to forget the nightmare that unfolded. The bereaved families were hopelessly trying to cope with the heartbreaking memories of their dead children and their funerals, but the trauma and grief remained undiluted.

After waking up to yet another sad morning, Janat Gul lay staring at the sagging ceiling for a moment. She quietly got up and stood on the verandah beneath the sweeping arms of the old mango tree.

The sky was now glowing pink reflecting the mild winter sun.

Sadly, she thought of how the wind would later arrive, denuding the tree. She wore a nondescript brown salwar kameez, now stained with stale tea, and the remnants of her last meal, quietly put on her black shawl, white-bordered, folded tightly about her head and pinned it under her chin as it shrouded her full body from head to toe. She gave a blank fleeting look at the empty verandah, then made her way out of the desolation of her house into the world outside, which was even more vacuous in its appeal. Janat slipped through the press of the crowded houses and down the trail at the corner of the dirt-filled Warsak Street, where the sidewalk began. Walking down the thoroughfare, toward the main entrance of the school, she crossed over the town's center, where a pompous Hakeem was giving a practical demonstration of his medicines. The Hakeem would get himself bitten on the wrist by a cobra snake, then rub ointment on it. In this way, he attempted to convince his audience that his medicine could protect them from death and harm.

She walked past him undisturbed, oblivious of the presence of the congregating crowd and the Hakeem, utterly indifferent to his miraculous offer. In her customary relationship with the world and its workaday folk, she did not take the slightest notice of anyone; in any case, she was not allowed to exchange glances, let alone stare, if she was to fulfill the patriarchal axiom. As she walked, she fell into a thoughtless trance, seemingly not even aware of the rise and fall of her own knees.

Cold and troubled, her eyes were only half open, carrying a faint, milky ring at the edge of the cornea, so often seen in people who have borne much in life. She appeared frail and delicate, both in stature and nature, marked by her tired appearance, her creeping gray hairs, and a hunched back. One could wonder how such a weak little body could bear so much labor, so much patience and pain.

She stared blankly at the poster on the school's exterior wall: *You are braver than you believe, and stronger than you seem.*

The wind whipped around her, and she hunched low against the wintry weather.

Her hand shook slightly as she stood patiently, huddled beneath her great black shawl. The school bell pealed; after a moment, a river of children flooded through the gates. Clad in green and grey parochial uniforms, they rushed, eager to be home. For once, the expression on her face was like that of someone dreaming a strange and lovely dream—a waking dream, with eyes open.

Through the sluice gates of her imagination, they all gushed out as one. Bright and dazzling faces like the face of the sun itself. An unknowable number of green and gray behind boots and winter coats emblazoned with a small emblem that carried an immensely powerful meaning:

I shall rise again.

Janat stared silently into space with her large, half-lidded eyes, her feeble fingers clutching the shawl close over her silvery hair. Children walked past, one after the other while she stood, time-bound and torn. A vision of him spun before her for a few dizzying seconds; instinctively, she raised her hand eagerly, but her mind quickly shook the image away as her senses reasserted themselves. And yet, she did not want the reverie to end.

The Armored Corps became aware of her presence, as she lingered long after most of the children were gone, staring silently at the now gloomy school.

"It's her, again," one whispered to the other, heaving a sigh.

"It has almost been a year, but Gul Bibi has not moved on."

"*Walahi,*[49] no! But how could she? He was their only son. The whole town knows that Allah Karim gave Hakeemullah a son, after fifteen years of marriage. He was the apple of Gul Bibi's eye." There was sorrow in the guard's voice.

"*Lalay,*[50] it may be years, may be a lifetime."

The guards approached her slowly. Janat Gul's eyes remained fixed on the gate. The children, long since gone, while she yet

---

49 Walahi: By God

50 Lalay: Friend

remained, unmoving, frozen in time, her hand hanging in midair like some forgotten marionette. The guard's voice cracked as it cut through the heavy silence.

"Gul Bibi, go home." The guards were familiar with her eccentricities, the look of confusion and grief in her dull eyes. She stood before them, a wisp of lost humanity with her wind-chafed skin.

"Go home? No, no," she protested, in a tiny, anxious voice. "I cannot go home—I must stay here. It would be terrible to leave him like this."

"Leave who, Bibi?" They already knew the answer, and what came next. Their gaze shifted from her wild eyes to her trembling hands, as she pulled out the black and white picture from her pocket. A boy. He looked ten, maybe eleven, wearing a striped shirt and a bow tie, a handsome little boy, with a slender nose, brown hair, and dark, slightly sunken eyes. He looked distracted, as though something had caught his attention just as the camera had flashed.

"Oho, Bibi, how many times have you been told—your son is a *Shaheed*,"[51] the guard implored. "You show us this picture every day. He is not coming back. Have patience, go home, Hakeem must be looking everywhere for you." The guards' pity for her was evident, even as they tried to shrug her off and compel her home.

---

51 Shaheed: Martyr

For a moment, one of the longest moments of Janat Gul's life, there was nothing but silence. It seemed to her one of the longest minutes of her life. *Patience?* She has heard that word all her life.

"You do not understand," she said quietly, assertively. "I must make sure I am always here when Zufash comes out. No one understands—that is why I did not tell anyone I was coming here. You see, I had to come, I promised him that if he's a good boy and goes to school today, then I will *cook matter palao*[52] for his supper. He loves it, it's his favorite dish, but only if I make it and feed him with my hands." She looked down. "These hands." Her eyes gleamed with tears—of unconditional love or utter despair, the guards could not decipher. "And so, *I* will wait for his return, right here, outside the gates. I *am* his mother, after all."

She patted her heart softly, as if to confirm her claim. She sat down and heard the lullaby she used to sing to him.

I'll wait, I'll wait
I love you like you've never felt the ache
I'll wait
I promise you don't have to be afraid
I'll wait
The love is here and here to stay

---

52 Matter palao: Rice and green peas

So lay your head on me

Your cradle is made up of pearls and flowers

Your face is shining like the moon,

Sleep, my child sleep,

I promise, you no longer have to be afraid

I'll wait, I'll wait

Oh Zufashay….my Zufashay….oh, mera beta[53] …

I'll wait.

53 Mera beta: My son

THE HOUSE OF MIRRORS

Khyber Pakhtunkhwa Police headquarters' Martyr's Desk processed compensation payments to the families' fallen victims of terrorism. Zufash's name was buried among a long list of those whose beneficiaries were awaiting money and other rewards promised to them for their loss since the attack happened, last year.

A team of district administrators met with the families one by one, negotiating their financial compensation. Some of the bereaved families took the money quietly, often due to their poverty, while others demanded a fact-finding inquiry, a commission headed by a senior judge to probe the attack. They demanded that the findings of that commission be made public. Their demands were nonetheless dismissed by the government, who claimed that the facts of the assault were clear. The terrorists just sought revenge from the Pakistan army for conducting the anti-terror operations in North Waziristan. A year has passed and yet, no judicial inquiry has been conducted into the security lapse at the school. Before the attack had happened, APS had been receiving threats. Of which we know now, the home ministry was well aware through the intelligence agency.

Grief-stricken parents sought vengeance, as most of the families were ethnic Pashtun, their lives infused with the tribal code of ethics in which *badal*—revenge—was a cornerstone. As such, they took grim satisfaction in knowing that the Pakistani army had wreaked its vengeance on the insurgents with hangings, arrests, and an offensive in the tribal areas where militants had previously operated with impunity. But those same parents railed against a deafening silence from authorities over how a security apparatus put in place to protect them could have failed their children so completely. The school was heavily guarded by the army, located within the cantonment. And, yet the attack took place and went on for nearly forty minutes. The parents wanted the facts, they demanded justice, not realizing that even though the arc of the moral universe was long, it so often bent toward injustice.

Salah Uddin Hussein, one of the district officers, came to visit Kaleemullah. The knock at the door was loud enough to stir a shadow awake. The old door, bleached by the relentless sun, creaked open after several knocks. Kaleemullah's face peered out of the dark, blinking confusedly at the brightness of the day and the unexpected guest it had brought.

"I am here from the Khyber Pakhtunkhwa Police headquarters, regarding Zufash," Salah Uddin told Kaleemullah, who nodded uncomprehendingly, opening the door wide. There was a charpoy inside, lined against the wall of the veranda. Against one wall hung a Persian prayer mat. Despite the sunlight streaming in through the open door, despite the whitewashed walls, gloom lurked in the corners of the thatched brick structure.

"How are you keeping up Kaleemullah, after Zufash's death?"

At first, Kaleemullah appeared reluctant to answer. It seemed a long time since his son's name had been spoken aloud by an outsider. And for the first time during that morbid afternoon, Kaleemullah left the room for a few minutes to regain his composure.

"I am here to give you the compensation check—will you please sign here, so I can go to the next house?" Salah Uddin said, seeming to be in a hurry.

Kaleemullah spoke in monosyllables, a distant look in his eyes. He was uncomfortable receiving the compensation. As a proud Pashtun, he was unsure how to equate a value to his son's spilled blood. "How much is it?" He clenched his jaw as he spoke, looking around uncertainty with red-rimmed eyes.

"Two million rupees, a lot of parents are still waiting in the line for this, you should not hesitate and take this without delay." Salah Uddin answered sympathetically.

"And you think this piece of paper will compensate for my Zufash's killing?" Kaleemullah pointed at the check indignantly. "Do you see these hands?" He extended his old and wrinkled hands towards Salah Uddin who nodded plaintively. "I carried my young son's lifeless body to his grave with these very hands. Do you think I cannot take care of my household? Not a day passes when my heart does not cry to hold my son in my arms—with every second, my eyes bleed for his return. What I have lost can never be reimbursed. My wife still goes to the school gate, staring at it blankly for hours on end. Still, she irons and washes his clothes, preparing breakfast and lunch for him. Still, she sings his favorite lullaby every night. Every moment of joy brings mourning to our home; be it Eid or a birthday celebration or anything else. My son's death continues to haunt us. I do not need your compensation! If you and your government cannot provide us justice, then know that Allah is just and He will reimburse us, rightfully.

"Kaleemullah, the government is trying..."

"Try...ing?" Kaleemullah stood up and looked into Salah's eyes.

"One soldier… only one soldier went in, after 144 lives were lost... before the contingent arrived. In a school, within the army compound, how was this even possible without connivance? You take me for a fool? Ah, Salah Uddin, you and your government and army's self-seeking house of mirrors with all its illusions of reparation and false justice can fool the world around and will surely win you laurels and earn you a good night's sleep. But know this; no one sleeps in this house, ever since I placed my son in his grave. We, along with our world, were buried along with him. You cannot buy us and never dare think that you can silence us with your money and awards. No one in this world can… Take it away!"

Salah Uddin stood quickly, surprised at the veracity of Kaleemullah's response, feeling suddenly ashamed as beads of sweat emerged on his forehead. He could not bear Kaleemullah's penetrating gaze any longer. He quietly stood up and left the room without a word, leaving nothing but silence and unrequited questions behind.

THE BECOMING

It was the ninth month of the Lunar Islamic calendar, the crescent moon appearing like a reedy fingernail through the cloudless wash of late morning sun, signaling the holy month of Ramadan. Even though almost a year and a half had passed since Zufash's death, still the penetrating silence in Kaleemullah's household had not lifted. The community had been offering emotional support to the bereaved families and life in Peshawar was slowly moving back to normalcy, but time seemed to have stopped for those who had lost their children and loved ones. No sympathies could awaken their heavy hearts. Even Zufash's pet parrot stood mute upon her perch as Janat performed her ablutions, quiet in her servitude.

As she knelt to pray her Fajar Salah, Kaleemullah sat beside her, and began reciting the Quran. Once they were both done, Kaleemullah broke the silence.

"Gul, it is a blessed month of Allah, and this was our son's favorite month. How eagerly he woke for suhoor, and how he loved the scent of your parathas. How would he put his lips to the jug of milk and take a long drink at iftar[54]—do you remember? If I listen hard, I still hear the echo of his voice, dancing along the walls of this house."

Janat nodded, but only slightly.

Kaleemullah did this often, attempting to strike a conversation with Janat, to console her aching heart. The topic always centered around Zufash, since Janat had no interest in anything else of the world; it was as if her mind could only understand the tapestry of his words if he weaved in that sound . . . his name—Zufash.

"You know what?" he said lightly, "how about you do not go to the gate today?" Fear swept through Janat's eyes, turning them blood red. "I mean to say," he corrected quickly, "I will take you to Zufash today. It is the start of our Holy month and . . . I know where he is! Allah willing. Would you like to go, Gul?"

---

54 Iftar: breaking the fast at sunset during Ramadan

he asked, gently.

Janat did not want to break her promise to wait outside the gates for Zufash. However, she also did not want to miss the chance of finding him elsewhere.

"I will come, Kaleemullah. I will come." Her voice rose slightly, creating a wave in her heart; a rising wave of hope.

At the break of dawn, Kaleemullah and Janat left their small concrete house, climbed on their scooter, and rode through the alleyways to the shining, wild prairie, its span, and glow in the morning light as vivid as a picture. There, an empty wind blew creaking trees against the gravestones. Many of the trees had been cut down, their trunks laid out in long rows like fallen soldiers on a battlefield. The dry smell of old stone filled the air, and weeds covered over the stones of the dead. The boundary that lined the path bloomed with wildflowers growing along the unkempt surface. Asymmetrical lines of graves, stretching for miles, created a dotted canvas of the land. Some crumbled against their centuries spent weathering in the harsh climate; others were smooth and shining, black writing against small slabs of marble laid with fresh flowers. Most, though were simply overgrown, as even those who once mourned had died themselves, and joined their brethren under the clay soil. Kaleemullah took Janat along the gravel path, wending through the maze of stones toward their son's final resting place.

How could a place be both so full and so empty at the same time? thought Janat, clad in a black and white *chaddar*[55] as she walked behind her husband. "Why have you brought me here, Kaleemullah?" she asked in a broken voice. He did not answer, but only gestured for her to follow. A few more steps and he stopped, stretching out his arm, pointing stiffly toward a mound of clay.

Slowly, she crept forward, to bear witness for the first time to her entire world now entombed in the earth. Amid the leaning and broken tombstones, the trampled mounds covered over with weeds was an epitaph, from the stone-cutter's album, that recalled her son's cherished name, followed by verses from the Holy Quran:

Inna lillahi wa inna ilayhi raji'un[56]
Zufash Uddin Kaleem
Date of Death: 16 December 2014
Age: 10 years

Janat fell to her knees before the small mound, laying her head upon the pillow of clay.

Kaleemullah's eyes glazed with tears. He knew well enough

---

55 Chaddar: Covering

56 We come from Allah and to him, shall we return.

that it was not favored, in any case—for women to visit graveyards in his culture, and this was one of the main reasons he had never taken Janat to visit their son. But in the two years that had passed since his death, she had shown no signs of recovery, and so he was forced to the decision, willing to grab hold of anything that might bring some hope, and some light back into their world. Anything that would bring her back from her obsessive, hopeless visits to the school, where she would never find him again. Kaleemullah left her there, walking back along the path to buy a wreath of fresh flowers from the small stall outside the graveyard, and to give his wife time alone with their boy.

She stared at the mound of clay, wondering how her son, who lived in a perpetual state of *wudu*,[57] could even exist in such a dark and dirty place. The surface of his grave carried an amber hue in the shining sun; beside it, a squadron of honeybees hovered drunkenly around an old bouquet of roses, slipping in and out of the flowers as if playing a game of hide-and-seek with her son.

"Praise be to my Allah, who alone can bless, for he never leaves one comfortless. And the earth-stained love you bore to him amid snares and temptations burning dim, so often weary, so often cold. He will repay it a thousand-fold."

She lifted her head up from Zufash's grave at the sound of

57 Wudu: Ablution

the old man's voice, speaking the verse as he entered carrying a walking cane from the other end of the graveyard, as though to himself. He might have been seventy, with a snow-white beard, a green plain kurta, and a green turban. How many had he seen into the ground? In a way, he looked like the end and the beginning himself—solemn and distant; godly. He wore no sandals, and as he wandered along the unkempt paths, he sprinkled drops of water over each clay mound he passed, as the rising heat of the day caused his wrinkled face to shimmer with beads of sweat.

"Life is but a roaming shadow, a pitiable thespian," he continued. "It is a tale full of trickery. A depressing truth. Beyond the reflection of a gold picket existence—a new grave." He murmured on as he passed by the burial mounds and gravestones, paying no attention to Janat's presence, turning his eyes here and there, everywhere but in her direction. As he approached Zufash's grave, he gave a small smile.

"Through starry crannies in his clay,
Grew bright and starry, more and more,
Where all had been dull earth before.
And through these chinks, unlike him not old
His soul converse high did hold,
With his one true love with mighty power

Who now bring him dewy fruits and flowers
From far heaven's groves and bowers."

He continued to chant as he gently sprinkled water over Zufash's grave; as he turned away, Janat called to him. "Baba jee! Did you know my son? Did you . . . bury him, here?" Janat asked plaintively. The old man returned a deep nod.

"Oh, I have buried them all. Grave after grave. The little ones yet the heaviest, entrusted to their earthen cradle. But know, your son does not dwell here! He never did," he said sternly, pointing at the grave.

"He is not there? But you said you buried him?" Janat stared up at him with red-rimmed eyes, confused.

"I did not bury your son! You did! Just like everyone else. Oh, I see it— first they bury, then they hurry back into the illusion until one day their own bodies are brought here. Thus, the circle of trickery continues."

Some might have said the old man's talk smacked of senility, but Janat had a feeling that he was perhaps more than what he appeared.

"I did?" she answered incredulously, touching her heart. "But I did not bury him. What are you saying, Baba Jee?"

"The truth, *bacha*![58] You buried him, you tore away his wings and imprisoned him for the sake of an illusion, instead of saving him. Do you think this dark prison of earth could hold the flowing light of life?" he said, pointing to the mound of clay. "A spirit of light will only drink the wine of light." He tapped his own heart. "Look for him in the blossoming of your heart, not in the wilting of his mold."

"I do not understand, Baba? What can a poor mother do? The pain is unbearable, those . . . *animals*, they shot him through the heart, spilled his blood like water. Who gave them or anyone in the world the right to take my *bacha* away from me? To inflict so much pain on a ten-year-old child? Who gave them the right to tear a mother's heart open? Savagely, they ripped his soul out from his little body, while my Allah watched. Lo! He watched, Baba, he simply stood by . . . tell me how I could ever come to terms with that? His throne did not shake and tremble in those moments. Why? Tell me why!" Janat choked on her words, grasping at her chest as if its contents might burst forth and spill out over Zufash's grave. It was only in this grief awakening moment that she had openly acknowledged her son's death. "I call him every day—I see him everywhere. Zufashay, my Zufashay! O my son, come back, for Allah's sake, come back! How will your

58 Bacha: Child

Amma live without you? Why? Why did Allah give a mother so much pain? Does He not have love in His heart . . . *for me*?" Janat cried openly, pounding at her chest with her fist, staring down at Zufash's grave, then casting her eyes skyward, into the heavens. With a sigh, the old grave digger set his bucket aside and sat beside her, placing a hand on her head.

"You are asking the Maker of love if he knows what love is? The Alif who created his beloved bay ب first and placed it right before his own Ism Allah (name of Allah) bestowing the gift of *Bismillah* upon us; you and the entire creation is the very proof of His divine mercy and love. We are all molded and knitted from the same essence, encapsulated safely in the dot of the Divine Bay that resides at the very feet of Allah's beloved, praising and bowing in his devotion in the eternal now.

Still, it was the prophet (peace be upon him) who was inflicted with the most pain by Allah.

Muhammad did not complain, for he knew that until a lover ceases to exist; he is not a lover. His love for the Divine was complete. And when Allah loved him back, he became his sense of hearing, and his sense of sight. He became the hand with which he gripped, the legs with which he walked. He became his heart, with which he loved all of mankind. Do not blame Allah for your lack of sight. Every love outside of *His* love is an attachment that is bound to bring forth pain. This world with all its grandeur, beauty and supplements promises you an oasis but imprisons you in a mirage, soon to end. The thirst will never end. The more you will pour; the thirstier you will get. Whilst the Divine countenance in you keeps you parched, only to pour His light into your cup, until you feel a river moving inside; until your very thirst replenishes you. Until all your duality collapses into the ever-flowing Nur[59] of Hu. Become it and be it.

Beti, death and pain are no more than an infinite comedy of illusion, just as this grave is no more than a prison for your mind. Use the key—believe in it—and Allah, the most gracious will open the door. You have within you both the sweet water and the jar that pours it. Let Him pour the light of your son into you. Let *Him* make you full. Do not grieve that your womb was softened with the pain of labor, for only then was the way created for your child to be born. Welcome your pain—only then will its cure find a way to your heart."

Janat thought over the man's words. "How can I find the key, Baba?" There came a lump in her throat, as a feeling of shame throbbed in her heart, threatening to pierce it.

The old man laughed gently. "Ah…You, just like all else have been sitting with it in your hand, all along," he replied, rising

59 Nur: Divine Light

slowly from the ground. "All this time, and yet you could not see. Because you have been blinded by the shape. Seek the shape of the glass and you will always remain thirsty. Seek the shapeless water and you will be filled to the brim forever. Trade the shadow cast by flesh and blood for the sun. Allah is the sun. Seek the sun, follow the river! Become His slave and you will find your king."

"Where should I start looking first, Baba?" Janat asks in a frightened voice, her eyes following him as he stood over her.

He laughed softly once again, nodding his head as if amused by her innocence. "Where does it hurt the most, Beti?"

Janat's clutched at her heart with both hands. "Here," she said with a sob.

"That is the center of your entirety," the old man nodded. "All that is resides within. You will find him where you left yourself! And when you do find him, call out to Allah: 'O Allah! *Istajib lana,*[60] *Ana 'l-'abd!*[61] '. Behold yourself to those words, remembering His response . . ." he paused, and bowed his head, smiling mysteriously. "And say a prayer, if you would, for this old grave digger."

With that, he took up his bucket and turned away, resuming his work, moving slowly as he sprinkled water over the graves,

---

60 Istajib lana: Answer me

61 Ana 'l-'abd: I am your slave

his back hunched, his bare feet dirty. As he left her, he whispered a new verse, his voice falling away as he disappeared behind an overgrown thicket of trees.

Ah! His royal soul wrapped in Allah's light,
Generous actions consecrate his mound,
more than all titles,
His is indeed, of Muhammadan sound.

An angel, a guide, or perhaps Khizir[62] - Janat considered, came to show her the way, soon to spread his wings and disappear. To her heart, he was no longer a poor and weary grave digger, just as the mound of clay before her was no longer her Zufash. No longer the measure of his height, but the eternal mountain of her submission. Not the epitaph of his memorial, the scrolling words on his tombstone, but his life force within her, flowing like a river. There was no other world but this one, no reality but what she had just experienced. Perhaps it was all a hallucination; if so, it was enough.

She stood quickly, wrapping her shawl tightly around her, and rushed out of the graveyard. She saw her husband's scooter parked

62 Khizir: In various Islamic and non-Islamic traditions, is described as a messenger, prophet, wali, slave, and angel, who guards the sea, teaches secret knowledge and aids those in distress.

outside, but she would not wait for his return. In that moment she cared for nothing but her burning intent. Her breath was uneven as she walked past it, her heart quivering in anticipation.

After walking the nearly two miles to Warsak Road, she arrived at the front gates of the school. It was almost home-time, and the street grew crowded with vendors and waiting parents. Finally, the moment arrived, and the gates were flung open, unleashing a torrent of children into the street. Janat stood quietly, her eyes closed, her heart open wide. As she held tightly to her very soul, her voice came in a slow whisper.

"O Allah! *Istajib lana, Ana 'l-'abd.*" (Answer me, I am your slave.)

"Anā al-Ḥaqq." (I am the Truth.) Her heart echoed.

"*Come, and see!*"

Amid the bustling of children, she saw him now, looking around anxiously, wearing his sparkling clean uniform. His curly strands of hair drifted over his small forehead. His water bottle hung from his neck. There, before her, in her awakened reality, in the arteries of a circling light that pulsed out from her—the light of the infinite. Janat tilted her head, beaming toward him the most beautiful smile in that perfect moment, a moment she'd thought lost forever.

She knelt and opened her arms wide.

"Zufash!" she shouted. "*Mera Beta*!"[63]

Their eyes met, and he smiled at her, her love for him reflected in her. He ran to her on small feet, pushing through the crowd, past the gate, piercing the bounds of reality, landing joyously in her arms. Janat embraced him tightly, her heart full. She picked him up, swaying with the euphoria of the moment, of a union drawn not from time, but of the purest love she'd ever known. "*I found you...I found you*!" She whispered in his ear blissfully. Drawn from her soul, into a vastness she'd never known, where there lived neither past nor future, but only Haqq. There, Janat had found her *truth*. And, in finding that, she finally found herself.

It was then that she knew the greatness of her life—of all lives—whatever she *loved*, she *became*.

---

63 Mera Beta: My son

EPILOGUE
THE MESSAGE

Divine Judgement (The Court of Allah)

Khaakzaad's Confession: My story is no longer indebted to the perseverance of being heard. My silence is my talk, my speechlessness is my speech. O Eternal Light! Trickle like tears from the eye of this moth. Head to foot suffering I am, full of longing is my story. It is true, indeed. I had the chances, while my victims had none. I killed them, point blank, without giving them the choice to fight back.

When the world pushed me to my knees, I had a thousand

ways to kneel and kiss the ground, there were a thousand ways to go home within, but I never truly attempted to be anything but the victim, who then became the victimizer. Truth was one and could not be otherwise. But I mistook the reflection for the mirror. The fault was mine and mine alone. All this time, Satan influenced my mind, but Allah dwelt in my heart. I never sought Allah within. Without struggle, there was no strength, but I gradually got lost in the blows and the pain, cast upon my earthen mold. Light was to enter through these wounds, I took the other path, I allowed darkness to creep through. I could have risen from the ashes, but I burnt the world around, instead. Thus, I am the message with words of warning written all over; for those led astray by the world made of dust and clay. A lesson that permeates and dominates the whole of man's existence, his society, civilization, and history. He is not what happens to him, he is what he chooses to become.

With the final call of the trumpet, Khaakzad hears a familiar voice, from the shadows opening the seal and announcing the judgment.

And here, the dust-clad boy is yet revealed,
His soul is withered—his doom is sealed.
There were hands once, that cherished his bloom,

Now he must lay low in his silent tomb,
And the mother's eyes that in pride once dwelled
On the beautiful form, she once loved so well,
Must sadly and mournfully turn away
From the cold, cold image of the senseless clay.
All is gone now; all is Khaak.
In the hellish dwelling, where darkness has set its mark.

Khaakzad gasps at the sight of the children appearing in the light. In Zufash's tiny hands, he holds the seven-sealed scroll; a title deed of Khaakzad's judgment, which now lay open. Khaakzad's eyes fall beneath Zufash's righteous gaze, and his head sinks lower with shame and lasting regrets. Khaakzad shall die a thousand times in this moment, only to be reborn a thousand times to witness this shame all over again, bearing it for eternity. His tale will disappear from the world's chronicles whilst Zufash's and all the childrens' starts, now...

"And Satan will say when the matter has been concluded,
"Indeed, Allāh had promised you the promise of truth.
And I promised you, but I betrayed you. But I had no authority
over you except that I invited you, and you responded to me.
So do not blame me; but blame yourselves.

I cannot be called to your aid, nor can you be called to my aid.
Indeed, I deny your association of me [with Allāh] before.
Indeed, for the wrongdoers is a painful punishment."
(Al-Quran: Ibrahim: Verse 22)

THE BEGINNING PREMISE

"A man stands here forever hell-bound for his sins. This slave seeks to speak---" An angel heralds the plea.

(All-pervading silence)

"----Why does this custom of silencing exist in your court? My tongue is tantalized to talk in your court, today. I will surely exhibit all of my hidden wounds today. Some fallen leaves were picked up by the tulip, some by the jasmine, some by the rose. My story is scattered around everywhere in your orchard. I am Khaakzad—the destroyer, the murderer, the sinner. I am a mere handful of scattered dust, but I do not know whether You or Your mirror or just dust and scum I ever were to be? Everything that I ever touched turned to dust and ceased to be. I was a skilled and heartless killer. And today, I will scatter around the same handful of dust in your blissful garden; hell-ridden, forever, for following in Satan's footsteps. But You did not create me as such—once, I was the ten-year-old Bahadur, son of a proud Wazir, the apple of my Morr's eye, a soulful confidante of my sister and a loyal friend to Your birds and cattle. I was once all things innocent and believed that a happy and peaceful life was possible in the world, You created.

That is, until Your garden's dwellers jointly robbed me away from my ingenious way. I was preached to my death with the word of life, my world snatched from my grasp. Why, O mighty Lord? What is the pleasure of living so in this world of Yours? Neither an eternal life, nor a worthy death was mine to be had. Whom happiness still mourns, that hapless person I am. Since eternity, destiny's pen has put me where all Your mourners are. Speech itself now sheds tears at my ill luck. My silent words, longing for an eager ear today, will You answer? Why would You merely sit and watch the suffering? Why would You let this injustice happen to mere children? Why don't You stop it? Where are YOU?" He bellowed in agony.

"Listen today, to the thunder of My Voice, O thoughtless one! The travail is yours and yours alone. A mere child who suffers and yet lives is to become wiser than the sages of his time. Schemes for man's destruction are afoot in Satan's lair since the advent of creation. Wisdom is man's redeemer. And, yet wisdom only comes from suffering. It bestows man with the discerning eye that sees everything, covered in illusions. It recognizes the exigencies of the nature of times. But what do men do with it? You remain entangled on the outside, engulfed in your own misery and victimhood. You continue to love the charm of material benefits and security, never seeing your own elegance in the mirror. Were you created to become a victim of your own ego? What did I hear? You blame everyone who inflicted this misery upon you? Give up intolerance O foolish one! In the earthly glass house, they are your own portraits which you have taken as the "other". Why did you conceal this sound of agony, and pathos in your pocket like a dagger, when alive? Those chosen to be wounded by Love do not roam in search of a cure. These wounded ones themselves create their own cure. Every woe's cure is to remain wounded with the sword of imperturbability. And the wound's remedy is to remain free from complaint. You are given the golden elixir of life, but with a choice; to either suffer to your full, only to become empty of self; and then, be free of all worldly afflictions. Or bind everyone to your hatred, your suffering and weigh yourself down until you could no longer stand your ground and crawl your way back here, to your beginning shamelessly carrying the idols of self-conceit. You ask, why all this pain? Pain in your heart is given to you, so you could become the embodiment of Light for others. To crack open your heart and expand it until it has the very room to house the eternal Truth.

If you are chosen to be the moth that burns, whose candle is setting you ablaze, do you not think? If you understand now, true sovereignty is veiled in this secret for man. Slavery is to remain imprisoned in the net of one's ego. Clarity of heart has nothing to do with external adornments or mere seeing or doing. Let Me ask you, what did you do, with that eye of sight, given to you? You couldn't even see your own reality in the cup of existence. Not only the earth, even the sky is lamenting your imprudence. You, who were to set others free through your suffering; you even made the Absolute in you, confined.

The cure for all ills and misfortunes is concealed in patience. Such is My design; My wisdom is not obligated to the scroll of existence. This is the law of Nature, this is the order of Nature. Those who are patient in suffering, are the beloved. Know this now, you are naught who you declared yourself to be. You remained lost, never to be found. You were placed on *the* path, but you failed to find youself. If you cannot find who you are, how can you reach Me? How can you know who I AM? Khaakzad could feel The Voice piercing through every echelon of his soul.

Khaakzad's damned and torn heart grieved on his failure. The earthly test had ended, so did his chance for absolution.

"Who am I? And, who are YOU?"

"In your grief-tormented land, the spell of hope *I Am*.
From your palpitating loud selfish desires,
the silent clamor *I Am*.
Embodiment of light is whose reality, that darkness *I Am*.
That small world of Bahadur,
whose sovereign ascendant yourself, *I Am*!
Neither wine, nor bearer, nor joy, nor chalice,
But the truth of everything in your existence' tavern, *I Am*.
An eternal treasure,
concealed in the wilderness of your dust, *I Am*.
Despite all odds, your Divine Purpose, *I Am*.
Who are *you*?
... *I AM*!"

***

A Dedication from Heaven

"O Mother, beyond the clouds,
Above people, beneath the skin, inside of you,
I am waiting to live again.
It was a pleasure to walk on the lines of your hand,
to feel the warmth of your cuddles,
and savor in the feeling of your adoration
as you kissed my being to life.
The toys you built that led us to laughter
Now they lead you nowhere
And when you arrive at nothing
You start right over
I smile, Mother.
My dirty clothes that
You have laundered
Exude my scent, still.
My blood-stained shoes that you have polished,
echo my tiny footsteps.
My room that you visit,
I still meet you there.

And when you scold me in thin air,
I smile, Mother.
You're just like me,
Forever hoping
Forever loving
Continue on your way,
your path decides mine,
your smile,
defines mine
Follow the line of your hand,
lead me to you, again.
Carry the soul of my universe in you, I reside,
like a secret treasure in you, I flow
like a thriving stream, treading my path to eternity.
Keep on walking,
I see you and smile.
I see you now, as you read.
I will see you when you think about these words.
My gaze captures your every move, your every word.
Say a word now.
Make a move.
I will smile as you read,
as your eyes forever gleam, thinking of me.
A fond kiss and then we sever,
A farewell—and then forever Deep in heart-wrung tears
I pledge to you beyond the clouds, we are *one.*

Beneath the skin, we are *one.*

Promise me today,
That you will not beg for the stilling of your pain,
that you will not cry in vain
That you will live on;
Joyous and sane

I am your ***heart****, mother.*

Make me ***live*** again.

***

GLOSSARY

Kalma Parh: to recite the Kalma

Abaya: covering

Aftaar: breaking of fast

Al-Arsh: Arabic word for God's throne

Alhumdulillah: praise be to Allah

Aloo Parahta: bread with potato stuffing

Allu keema: an eastern dish of meat and potatoes

Amma Jan: beloved mother

Ana 'l-'abd: I am your slave

(as): abbreviation of Alayhi al-Salaam, meaning "peace be upon him." Often appears following names of prophets to demonstrate respect.

APS: Army Public school

As-salamu alaykum: peace be upon you

Baba: father

Bacha/bachem: child

Bakhuda: by God

Baigairat: shameless

Baraat: wedding procession

Beta/mera beta: son/my son

Beti: daughter

Bibi: lady

Biryani: indo pak rice dish with potatoes and meat

Bismillah: in the name of Allah

Chaarpayi: a traditional woven bed used in the Indian subcontinent

Chand sitara: moon and star

Chapatis: bread

Chadors: a large piece of cloth that is wrapped around the head and upper body leaving only the face exposed, worn especially by Muslim women.

Cholha: stove

Da'wa: invite

Edhi: a charity-run organization by Abdul Sattar Edhi, begun in Pakistan, providing ambulances, shelter, and support.

Eid: Muslim celebration holiday after the month of Ramadan

Fateha: first Qur'anic verse in Muslim's holy book

Fajr azan: Morning call to prayer

Fajr salah: Morning prayers

Fi Aman Allah: in God's safety

Hajar/Hajirah: wife of Ibrahim (as) and mother of Ismail (as) to be remembered for all time

Her Sunnah (The word Sunnah is an Arabic word meaning "tradition" or "way." For Muslims, Sunnah means "the way of the prophet". The Sunnah is made up of the words and actions of Muhammad, the prophet of Islam. Muslims believe Muhammad's life is a good model for them to follow in their own lives.) is an integral part of an obligatory pillar of Islam, the Hajj (Holy Pilgrimage to Mecca) Named Hagar in the Bible.

Halwa Poori: a sweet savory with bread

haqq: truth

Ibn-insaan: humankind

Inna lillahi wa inna ilayhi raji'un: We come from Allah and to him shall we return.

Inshaa Allah: God willing.

Istajib lana: Answer me.

Kalma: a word, speech, saying, discourse, part of speech; the Islamic confession of faith (i.e., lā ilāha illa′l-lāh, meaning, "There is no god but God and Mohammad is the prophet of God.").

Kalma eh shahadat: the chanting of Kalma in a funeral procession

Khabees: rascal

Lalay: friend

Lassi: drink made from yogurt milk

Lassi walla: The shopkeeper selling butter milk

Madrasah: school for religious teachings

Makh Katal: unveiling of one's face, usually done by a woman relative

Masher: head of the clan

Maulana: cleric

Mera Chanda: my moon

Mor: mother

Mujahedeen: Religious Fighters

Murshid: guide, teacher

Odreka: stop there

Pakol: Peshawari hat. Paratha: bread

Pathan: a member of a group of Muslim people from Afghanistan and northwest Pakistan

Pehal dooj: a local game

Pulao: rice dish with chicken or vegetables

Purdah: the practice in certain Muslim and Hindu societies of screening women from men or strangers, especially by means of a curtain

Qahwa: green tea

Rasool: alarabic word for messenger, apostle

Reham: mercy

Roti: bread

Rukhsati: a "sending off" that takes place when the groom and his family leave together with the bride.

Sahib: a polite title or form of address for a man

Sama da: Pashto word for okay

Shabashay: well-done

Shalwar kameez: pakistan national dress

Shemagh: headdress fashioned from a square scarf, usually made of cotto

Shehnai: wedding music instrumental

Sher: lion

Suhoor: morning breakfast before fast

Surah: a chapter in the Quran

S-wing: a secret organization within ISI, largely composed of retired military and ISI officers. Does not exist officially, manages relations with radical elements.

Pashto: the language of the Pashtuns, which belongs to the Iranian group. It is the official language of Afghanistan and is also spoken in northern areas of Pakistan.

Pattu: A kind of woolen fabric used to make Pakol hats

Tanga walla: driver of a two-wheeled, horse-drawn vehicle.

Tesbih: prayer beads. Also called "misbaha."

Wadu: ritual washing

Walahi: by God

Wruna: brothers

Zabardast: excellent

-zad: son of, a suffix to a name in farsi: Khaak-zad

Zuhr: muslim afternoon prayers

ABOUT THE AUTHOR

MAHDI is an own voice author, whose sole purpose is to shed light on the quintessential aspects of duality and oneness in all that exists. That adds such an authentic touch to *Khaak*; a moving story, based on true events entailing the attack on the Army Public School in Peshawar, Pakistan that devoured the lives of more than 144 children and teachers by the alleged Terrorist organization called TTP(Tehrik-i-Taliban) on December 16, 2014. To pen this tale of sorrow and cruelty became more of a conscious decision for Mahdi; to re-create a story-world that didn't necessarily begin with screams and end in silence, but roared with the "love" of a mother and the earth shattering spirit of a valiant seven-year-old, declaring and honouring a growing presence, the presence of a message that has not been said, but which is very much there.

The message in *Khaak* does not intend to present things through the cold-eyed lens of factuality, rather it encourages the readers to listen to the voice, of unexpressed feelings and emotions and give a real wrought out design of Zufash's and Janat Gul's message; about the spirit of unconditional love, about rising again from the ashes, about the future, as it flourishes under the mantle of books and childhood galore.

"MAHDI is my conscious choice as it resonates with my soul purpose.

MAHDI means guidance, it means, voice against injustice, it means a higher consciousness that transcends the boundaries of limitations, pain, suffering and transforms all into growth, love and light!!

MAHDI is sheer alchemy of the soul."

Indeed, *Khaak*'s message is the same just as the essence of the name Mahdi, to transcend the suffering and pain, to become one with the collective energy of love and healing, to make conscious choices for a better earth for us and our children, to simply exist in peace and harmony with all that is called "life!" Mahdi and *Khaak* resonate that Oneness, of purpose.

ABOUT THE ARTIST

The Cover , "Timeless Eye of Eternity" is meticulously designed by a young 12-year-old aspiring artist Nuha whose timely contribution through the use of her creative imagination for *Khaak* adds such a unique and original nuance to the relationship entailing this art piece and the story itself. Since *Khaak* portrays the very dreams and inspiration of children, it is most befitting that someone as young as Nuha drew this heartening cover for *Khaak* inspired by the spiral as a timeless and immortal archetypal form that which is often found beneath the surface of all things in nature and the universe.

Global Voice's logo is inspired from the ancient drawings of the Kalahari San Bushmen scattered across Southern Africa upon the rocks, walls and caves. And from their wise prophecy: "When the Little People of the Kalahari dance, then shall the Little People around the world dance, too." 10 percent of Khaak's sales will benefit other authors, igniting this dance throughout the globe. www.globalvoicefoundation.com

Since IML's humble erratic beginnings, the graphic symbol of the Mantis mascot has reverently danced across our newsletters, our logo, the watermarks of the website, the original interiors of our books, and now throughout this book. The hunter, the trickster god, the praying mantis is known to shoot arrows of truths through the magical stories of the Kalahari Bush-men-and-women. For as long as they can remember, Mantis has been auspiciously inspiring the mythological myths of these First People, the hunter-gatherers who nomadically walk the earth whenever they can, as our nomad authors write their way through life on the borders of civilization.

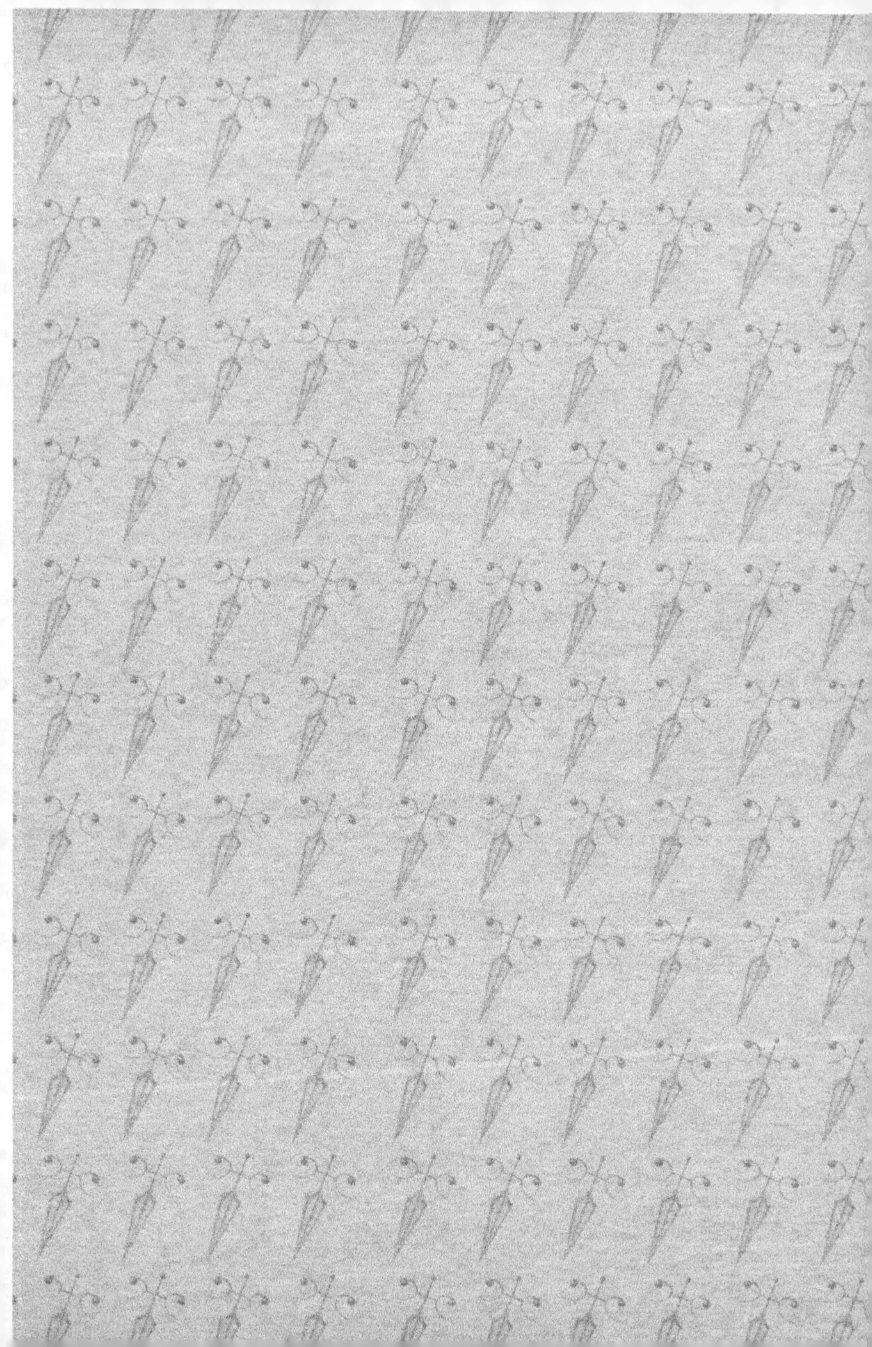